By Janet Litherland

Novels

Worth Dying For
Sweet Justice
The Long Road Home
Song of the Heart
Vanished
Chain of Deception
Discovery in Time

Nonfiction Books include:

Broadway Costumes on a Budget
Absolutely Unforgettable Parties
The Complete Banner Handbook
Storytelling from the Bible
Getting Started in Drama Ministry
The Clown Ministry Handbook
Everything New and Who's Who in Clown Ministry

Praise for the Author

[Litherland's] books are morally pure and her style of writing captivates audiences, showing this type of writing can be accepted and enjoyed without defilement. ... [She] knows how to animate her characters with realism. –Clark Isaacs, *Clark's Eye on Books*

Litherland's authentic characters and careful research succeed brilliantly. ... To merely hold my reader's curiosity is never enough, but to grip my heart with honest enchantment is a true joy. –Arthur L. Zapel, Chairman of the Board and former Executive Editor/Publisher, *Meriwether Publishing Ltd.*

Janet Litherland skillfully integrates authentic pieces of history, allowing us to feel the time and place of her story. –Patricia Sheehy, author of *Veil of Illusion* and *Field of Destiny*

Intriguing but credible characters and attention to period detail; these are what make a good historical novel. Janet Litherland knows how to craft both. –Ken Libbey, author of *Vantage Points* and *Midnight in Prague*

WORTH DYING FOR

A Story of Courage and Consequence

Janet Litherland

Author Photo by Dyess-Tidwell Studio

ISBN 978-0-7414-8345-4

Printed in the United States of America

Published March 2013

INFINITY PUBLISHING
1094 New DeHaven Street, Suite 100
West Conshohocken, PA 19428-2713
Toll-free (877) BUY BOOK
Local Phone (610) 941-9999
Fax (610) 941-9959
Info@buybooksontheweb.com
www.buybooksontheweb.com

Chapter 1

Meadow Bridge, Georgia—2002

A bullet whistled past Hannah Rosse's ear as she crossed the living room of her home. It knocked a framed photo off the mantle, and sent it crashing to the floor. Hannah jerked reflexively and moved quickly without panic. She did not scream. The bullet had entered through an open window. There'd been no report from the gun, just the quick "chuff" sound made by a silenced weapon—a familiar sound, a sound all too prevalent during Hannah's younger days.

Standing away from the window, she considered what had just happened. *If they had intended to kill me,* she thought, *they would not have missed. It was a warning ... this time.* In fact, it was the only such "warning" she'd had in years. Someone knew who she was. Someone knew *where* she was. And she could not call the police.

Hannah had opened the window earlier to let in fresh air and sunshine. Now, she closed it and turned back toward the fallen photo. It was very old, sepia-colored, and protected by a mat that had kept the glass from touching it directly. She retrieved it from among the shards, just slightly damaged, and gratefully and lovingly held it to her heart. Her parents, Eli and Ada Rosenthal. ... The photo, her only memento of a life that never was.

~~~~~

Later that day, as the sun began to set, Hannah relaxed comfortably on the front porch of her Victorian-era home, unafraid. She was bold, and she was smart. She also was a youthful sixty-nine years old and shunned what she called "old-lady clothes." To her, comfort meant Capri pants, T-shirt and sandals.

On this particular evening, the breeze was comfortably cool, the lemonade in her hand was tasty, and the only thing on Hannah's mind other than (and in contrast to) the gunshot, was how blessed she felt. She'd been living happily here in Meadow Bridge for nearly thirty years. Whatever happened now, she had no regrets.

As she sipped her lemonade, a strange car pulled up and stopped on the street in front of her house. It was a sleek, black sedan. Two men inside. Hannah carefully set her glass on the small table beside her chair, stiffened her back, lifted her chin, and instinctively closed her fingers around the weapon in her pocket—a special knife that had been her constant companion for many years. Some habits never die.

The passenger got out and started up the walk toward the porch; the driver remained in the car. And Hannah felt a sudden wave of dread—not fear, but dread—because, without knowing who he was, she recognized the gait, the demeanor, the clothing, the *look*. It all belonged to her past. *Belonged* in *her past, damn it!* What could he possibly want? Was his objective connected to this morning's gunshot?

He stopped at the foot of the steps. He was young and hesitant. *Probably inexperienced*, Hannah thought. *First assignment?*

"Good afternoon, Mrs. Rosse," he said.

"It's *Ms.*"

He carefully placed one foot on the bottom step. "*Ms.* Rosse," he said, "my name is John Jackson."

"Sure it is."

He didn't reply, but his brow furrowed slightly.

"I don't need to know who you are," Hannah said, her gaze unwavering, "because I know *what* you are. Why are you here? This house—my *life*—is off limits!"

He straightened his shoulders, put both feet firmly on the ground, and looked at Hannah without blinking. His training had apparently kicked in. "May I join you on the porch," he said, a statement rather than a question.

Hannah considered for what must have seemed an eternity to the unwelcome visitor. Then, grudgingly, she indicated the chair on the other side of the small table. He would be able to reach it without crossing in front of her. With her hand still in her pocket, fingers still wrapped around her knife, she watched him slowly seat himself. A quick glance toward the car noted the driver talking on a cell phone.

The young man put his empty hands on the table in full view and turned to face her. "You can relax, Ms. Rosse, and can even take your hand from your pocket. I'm not going to hurt you."

"Damn right, you're not; and my hand stays where it is. State your business."

He shrugged. "You're being called back for one last job."

"Impossible."

"We need you."

"We?"

"Your former employers." Then he uttered a code phrase that left no doubt about who or what he represented. "This is something only you can do, Ms. Rosse. You're uniquely positioned for it."

"No."

"… No?"

"You heard me. It's been thirty years since I came in from the cold. Thirty *good* years! And I have no intention of going back out there." Her voice had taken on the edge of hard steel. "I *like* my present life. I've *earned* it."

"You must at least come in for a briefing. I believe that when the mission is explained, you'll change your mind."

3

She looked at him as if he were a drooling idiot. "In just a few months I'll be seventy years old, for heaven's sake!"

"But you look, and move, like a woman twenty years younger."

"If that's a compliment, I'm not flattered. My skills are rusty and so is my brain. I don't *think* like I used to!"

"The job is already planned, Ms. Rosse. You won't have to think. Just do it."

Hannah lifted her chin even higher. "... That is definitely *not* a compliment."

He couldn't quite stifle a little smile. "Your briefing is tomorrow morning," he said. "Ten o'clock." He named the place.

"And if I choose not to attend?"

He leaned in toward her, all trace of smile gone, and told her what would happen to the nice, comfortable life she presently enjoyed.

"Oh, stop! Those juvenile bully tactics won't work with me. I've been around too long for that!"

He sat up and cleared his throat, suddenly looking like a frightened little boy. "Are you willing to risk it, Ms. Rosse?" he asked.

And Hannah knew immediately that his fear wasn't for her. It was for himself. He would not be permitted to fail. She recalled an occasion when she was his age and circumstances had put the same fear into her. She felt sorry for him. After all, he wasn't the enemy. She also was curious. What kind of job? And why? Hannah rose quickly to her feet and looked down at him, staring so hard it was as if she'd slapped him. This forced him to rise too, though his move was wary. She smiled inside as she watched him, and told herself, *It's all about power*. Then she said aloud, more sharply than intended, "Leave now, Mr. ... John Jackson." Couldn't help rolling her eyes at the obvious alias.

She had not said she would attend the briefing, but he knew she was thinking about it. "I'll pick you up," he offered.

4

With fake sweetness she said, "I asked you to leave, Mr. Jackson." Then she shouted, "Now!"

He straightened his shoulders and turned away with a nod and a half-smile. He was fairly certain he had aroused her curiosity and accomplished his mission. Nevertheless, his fingers were crossed as he strutted down the steps.

She watched him walk to the waiting car, watched as the car drove away. Of course she was considering the message he'd delivered. And, she knew that *he* knew she was thinking about it—her brain wasn't *that* rusty! Plus, she really was curious. What in the world could they want with her? And why was she "uniquely positioned"?

Meadow Bridge was the kind of town where one could always see a familiar face. Each day she saw children on their bicycles and waved to neighbors who had become friends, including some who walked by for exercise and often stopped to talk. From her front porch, Hannah enjoyed looking at the pretty yards and flowers across the street, especially Suzy Carlson's colorful roses. They were bright and cheerful and made her smile. She found comfort in familiar surroundings. Seeing it all there at the close of each day was peaceful, reassuring, and never ceased to amaze her. She couldn't possibly be "uniquely positioned" in Meadow Bridge, of all places! Should she risk losing the life she'd grown to love, for an unknown job? Or would the job *save* her peaceful life?

Hannah Rosse had already lived more fully than most people on the planet. She'd known great adventure. She'd been everywhere in the world she'd ever cared to go and done everything she'd ever wanted to do, in addition to things she wished she'd *never* done. Though she'd believed with all her heart—and still believed—those acts were for the greater good, some of the memories were painful. To balance those memories, she knew that in later years she had made a positive difference in the lives of those around her, and that meant everything. Life was good.

Why should I put myself in danger again? ... Her curiosity argued with her common sense for the next twenty minutes.

Finally, she made a decision. She would go to the place John Jackson had cited in Macon, Georgia, and listen to the briefing. Yes, she would listen. And if she didn't like what she heard, she'd tell them exactly where they could put their *problem*!

Chapter 2

At 10:00 the next morning, Hannah—dressed in an attractive burgundy business suit that enhanced her slim figure and her intimidating posture—arrived at an upstairs office in Macon, a city four times the size of Meadow Bridge. The sign on the door read, "Geology Consultants." *Well*, she thought, wryly, *that certainly discourages drop-ins.*

Two people greeted her. One was a man, probably in his late forties, with close-cropped gray hair. He was tall and slim but looked extremely fit. The other was a younger woman, a little on the chunky side, with black-framed glasses she kept pushing up on her nose, and a frosty smile with attitude. After they were seated at a small conference table, credentials were established, and the two smiled and said they preferred to be addressed as "Doc" and "Laura."

Their guest did not smile. "You may call me Hannah," she said.

Doc was clearly in charge. "This should be an easy job for you, Hannah," he said.

"If it's so easy," she replied, her eyes locked on his, "get someone else to do it."

Laura pushed her glasses up on her nose and said, "No one else is as—"

"Uniquely positioned?" Hannah finished, mimicking John Jackson's words and tone of voice.

"Exactly," Doc answered, "because you're on site. Our suspect lives in Meadow Bridge."

"What! Meadow Bridge is an innocent little town full of good people. There couldn't possibly be anyone living among them devious enough to interest the Agency."

Laura smirked. "You're there, aren't you?"

Doc gave Laura a look that clearly conveyed, *Shut up,* then he said, "I'm afraid it's true, Hannah, and since you're a long-time resident, involved in the community, with plenty of friends and acquaintances—contacts—you *are* uniquely positioned. Sending a stranger in would be a huge mistake. Face it: Meadow Bridge is one of those Podunk hamlets where everyone knows everyone else's business. Too risky."

Hannah was incensed. "Yes, we know one another, but we don't *pry.* And our town is hardly Podunk—there are a lot of cultural and charitable activities going on!"

"Okay, okay. I apologize. Which is something I rarely do," he added, looking her straight in the eye. "We *need* you, Hannah."

She folded her arms across her chest. "Is that why you sent the sniper to my house yesterday morning? To put me on alert? To let me know the Agency would come calling?"

Doc appeared stunned. He leaned forward. "What do you mean, a *sniper*? What happened?"

"You didn't send him?"

"Absolutely not! Tell me about it."

So she did, ending with, "It was a pro, obviously trying to scare me, which he—or she—did not."

"Even more reason, now, to put you on this mission. For *your* safety as well as that of others."

Still angry but even more curious, she asked, "So, what's the problem and what's the plan?"

"The problem is something you've excelled at in the past—tracking spies and collaborators. There is no plan, other than 'observe and report.' The process is up to you; the consequences will be handled by others. Just use your charms—your *talents*—and gather information on one particular person."

Now it was Hannah's turn to smirk. "And who do you think might possibly succumb to this old lady's demon charms?"

"Martin Wynn."

Hannah felt as if the breath had been sucked out of her system. "You've got to be kidding! You're asking me to betray a friend. A very good friend! I've known Martin since he and his wife—late wife, now—arrived in Meadow Bridge a few years ago. We both volunteer at the local food bank!" She took a deep breath and placed her *fists* firmly on the table. "And since you've been snooping, of course you would know that Martin and I have been out to dinner together."

Doc inclined his head. "As I said, you're uniquely positioned."

"Are you suggesting Martin is behind the gunshot?"

He shrugged, and Hannah shuddered. She abhorred his attitude—the same attitude she, too, had proudly embraced all those years ago. "Martin would not do that to me. So, what do you expect me to find by prying into his privacy?" she asked.

"We think he's a sleeper."

"Ridiculous! What brought you to that conclusion?"

"A tip."

"Reliable?"

Again, Doc shrugged. Such *tips* usually came from defectors, and Hannah simply could not get her mind around that possibility. "I think you're dead wrong," she said.

"Prove it." His eyes seemed to look straight into her brain, and a hint of smile tugged at one corner of his mouth. "Take your time with this one, Hannah. You know what to do."

Yes, she knew. She'd done it before, but she was much younger then. With her talent for acting and manipulating, not to mention her youthful beauty, she'd uncovered more than one sleeping foreign agent. Of course there were times when she'd had to appear wild-eyed, dirty and smelly. For those jobs, she'd enhanced her persona with gleanings from dumpsters and garbage cans!

But then one day she was sent to Scranton, Pennsylvania, where she impersonated a college student who had recently lost her father. She inserted herself into the life of a very nice older gentleman, a father figure. She shared her sad story with him—a cover story, of course—and gained his trust, meeting with him often to discuss her (fake) problems. She liked the man very much but felt no guilt for misrepresenting herself. She was doing her job. She did it well, too. She proved beyond a doubt that he was *not* a sleeper! And she'd do it again. She would arrange to see Martin Wynn more often and enjoy every minute of it!

~~~~~

In Hannah's other life, as she now thought of her past, she had always been an active agent, never a "sleeper" who was planted deep, waiting to be activated. Sleepers often waited many years, ingratiating themselves into communities, gaining the trust of unsuspecting friends. Is that what Martin had done when he'd moved to Meadow Bridge? Did this little town mean no more to him than a convenient place to hide, to wait? Was Hannah one of his unsuspecting friends?

Actually, Hannah and Martin had been out to dinner several times; they'd also gone to a few movies together. And when Glen Campbell visited the nearby town of Perry last month, they attended his concert. Martin had been easing the loneliness she'd begun to feel lately. Not the same kind of loneliness she'd felt as an agent. Then, she was always alone. Even with acquaintances she was alone. Sometimes the loneliness had hurt deeply, but she'd learned to push it aside, to avoid thinking about it.

Being in Meadow Bridge was different. She was surrounded by real friends, not mere acquaintances. They'd celebrated with her at her marriage to David Spencer, and they'd been there for her four years later when he passed away. Now she only felt truly lonely in the evenings, when a good book or television program simply was not enough. She craved companionship. And Martin Wynn had begun supplying it. He was bringing a special happiness into her life. Was it all a lie?

Last year Martin appeared at the gym where Hannah worked out weekday mornings with a group of "seniors." He joined the class a short time later. And a few weeks after that, he became a food bank volunteer. He was ten years younger than Hannah; but Hannah, who was extremely fit, looked and moved like a woman ten years younger than Martin. John Jackson had been right about that! If she'd wanted to, Hannah could have developed an exercise program that would put Jane Fonda to shame. No question.

Hannah was angry. Not at Martin, but at Doc and Laura for poking a hole in her happiness, for planting doubt in her mind. Yes, she would take this ridiculous assignment, if for no other reason than to prove them wrong!

~~~~~

Who is Hannah Rosse, really? When I'm gone, will anyone ask? Will anyone care? I've lived the last thirty years of my life in a small town in middle Georgia, pleasantly if unremarkably. My first nearly forty years were vastly different—different name, different appearance, different way of speaking. No one here knows about my former life. They don't know that English is not my native tongue, though no one would ever guess. I speak it fluently and with a bit of southern accent, which blends well with the voices around me. Nor do they know that my special skills enabled me to accumulate a small fortune that only my favorite charities will ever see. They don't know me, really.

Most people would consider a sixty-nine-year-old woman elderly, but I'm not the least bit infirm, and I still have my wits about me. The time has come to tell my story, to disclose the truth, to come clean. That's an odd expression, isn't it?

Janet Litherland

"Come clean." Is that how I'll feel when life is over? Clean?
Or will I go to my grave feeling dirty, dirtier than ever?

Chapter 3

Germany and the Netherlands—1940

For Hannah Rosse the early years in Germany, where she was born Heide Rosenthal, were all about survival. Her German mother and Jewish father had married in 1931, before the Nuremberg laws were passed prohibiting such marriages, and Heide was born the next year. As a child, she knew about war because she and her parents lived with it every day. Average folks in Germany had no control over their situation and were just as frightened as Hitler's enemies. Propaganda was a powerful weapon, and the German people risked prison if they listened to foreign broadcasts. Even at a young age, Heide's father had taught her about guns and how to shoot. And her multilingual parents had insisted she learn English along with German. "Knowing more than one language may someday save your life," her mother had said.

The middle years were more about adventure than survival as Heide—then known as Hanne Smit—accepted, then embraced, her situation. She was smart. She learned quickly, attaching images, thoughts, ideas and words to her brain for later retrieval. She also discovered she could adapt to her surroundings like a chameleon—a sweet, innocent young girl one minute and a foul-mouthed guttersnipe the next. She easily assumed a variety of identities, depending on the circumstances, or rather the *requirements* of the day.

As she grew into her early twenties—skilled, fit and agile—the attractive young woman was able to accomplish unspeakable things under the guise of righteousness and honor, quickly and without detection. She was action-oriented, motivated and fearless, refusing to be intimidated. This boosted her status with those who depended on her for survival, and garnered the admiration of her peers. In the early days of the CIA, most women worked in low-level jobs or in support of men who worked as field agents. Some of the "old boys" were resentful when qualified women such as Heide Rosenthal/Hanne Smit (now officially known as Charlotte "Charley" Stowne) began earning places in their ranks. But *this* woman never cowered; she stood up to them.

However, by 1971 in America, when Klansmen were bombing school buses in Michigan, scholars were poring over *A Theory of Justice* by John Rawls, people were flocking to movie theaters to see *The French Connection*, and teenagers were bouncing to The Osmonds' *One Bad Apple*, the lifestyle that Heide/Hanne/Charley had found adventurous, if questionable, had lost its appeal. She was almost forty years old, craving the life she had never been able to have—a home, a husband, at least one child before it was too late, and a peaceful and loving existence. In other words, the life her mother had hoped to have before all hope was taken away.

Retirement—the beginning of life as Hannah Rosse.

~~~~~

"But it's too soon to leave, Mutti," the child said to her mother. She spoke in German, her native tongue. "Papi isn't back yet. I can't go to Tante Elsa's without saying goodbye to Papi!"

Heidi's father, Eli Rosenthal, had been gone for two days. He was not coming back, not ever. And his German (Aryan) wife could not bear to tell their only child that he had been taken away by the Nazis.

"I'll be joining you in a few days, Heide. Papi will find us. He knows where we'll be." Ada Rosenthal nearly choked on the lie but vowed to herself that she would tell Heide the truth as soon as they were together again. They would be safe in Amsterdam with Ada's sister and niece. "We can't stay here another day. It's too dangerous. We've talked about this before, Heide. Even though I'm German—and you look like me, with your fair skin and light brown hair—our name is Rosenthal. It's Jewish. Your father is Jewish, and that means trouble for our family. We have to leave now, and we can't go on the same train."

The school children had heard the man who yelled on the radio. They knew that he was the leader of their country, the Führer, who demanded obedience. Now they must greet people by saying "Heil Hitler," rather than *Guten Morgen* (Good Morning). They thought that was dumb, but they knew better than to express themselves outside their own little circle.

Heide dreaded the separation from her mother, but she sensed Mutti's fear and knew she was acting out of love. She, too, was frightened; but, more than anything, she wanted to please Mutti. She held her favorite stuffed animal—a spotted dog with perky ears—closer to her body and looked up at the nice lady from Holland, a province in the Netherlands. The lady, who smiled encouragingly, had arrived to take her to the train station and accompany her across the border. She carried only a small handbag containing a few family photos (one of which included a young girl who resembled Heide) and Dutch paperwork identifying Heide as Hanne Smit, a Dutch citizen. Both she and the papers had been supplied by an organized rescue group Eli Rosenthal had contacted before his abduction.

"You must do whatever it takes to survive," Heide's mother insisted, kneeling so that her face was level with Heide's. "Promise me!" And the bewildered eight-year-old displayed the courage of an eighteen-year-old. She lifted her chin, kissed her mother firmly on the cheek, and promised.

Ada Rosenthal was determined to save her only child. She wanted her far away from what she saw as the Nazi plan for Jews: *Vernichtung durch Arbeit und Hunger*—death by hard work and little or no food.

Later, as the train pulled away from the station, Heide shed a single tear, but it was a big one. She didn't know it then, but that tear was for her mother, her father, the town, the home, the school, and her friends—all of which she would never see again.

~~~~~~

Ada Rosenthal was arrested that same night for "harboring Jews," which stripped her of her tenants' rights. She was sent to a concentration camp. Heide had escaped just in time.

For many of the children rescued by the anti-Nazi resistance, survival meant living with strangers in foster homes, often shuffled from one home to another. Heide was fortunate. She was taken to Amsterdam to the home of her aunt, Elsa Smit, a widow with a daughter Heide's age. Elsa and Trudi welcomed her with smiles and hugs, addressing her by her new Dutch name.

"Hanne, we are so glad you are here and safe," said Elsa, speaking in English. "I have a nice hot meal waiting for you. I'm sure you are hungry, yes?"

"Yes! Thank you, Tante Elsa. I'm also happy to be off that noisy train, but the lady who brought me was very nice."

"Hanne, you already know how important it is to keep your new name, Hanne Smit. Your former name must never be spoken again."

Hanne nodded obediently. "The nice lady told me. She wouldn't let me say a word during the journey. I had to smile and pretend I was very shy."

They settled around the table, and the two little girls began talking about dolls and other things that interest children. Suddenly Trudi reached over and gently stroked her cousin's hair. "I like your hair," she said, shyly. "It's pretty that way." Hanne had light brown bangs that dangled just above her eyebrows.

"The nice lady cut it in the bathroom at the train station," Hanne said. "She told me it had to match the girl in the picture she brought with her, but I really couldn't see the girl very well. There were some other people in the picture and it was kind of blurry. I hope Mutti likes my hair." She turned to her aunt. "Tante Elsa, how long will it be before Mutti gets here?"

Elsa tried to smile. "I don't know, dear, but I hope soon." And she was hoping fervently. This war had brought nothing but sorrow and uncertainty to loving families.

"And Papi? What about Papi?"

"We can only wait and see."

Meantime, at Elsa's suggestion, the girls amused themselves with languages. Hanne, Elsa, and Trudi already spoke excellent English. Though Elsa had grown up speaking German, she had not passed that language on to Trudi. So, Trudi taught Hanne basic Dutch phrases in exchange for German. After practicing for three weeks, they began, awkwardly, to converse. Elsa assured them they would improve quickly. In Hanne's case, she insisted. "It is fortunate, Hanne," she said, "that you have your mother's coloring and can pass as non-Jewish. Now, the sooner you master the Dutch language, the safer you will be. Oh, and it is just fine to call me *Tante* Elsa, because *Aunt* translates the same in both German and Dutch."

Hanne was well aware of the need for security and she was a quick learner. To the neighbors, she was introduced as a relative of Elsa's late husband, Arne Smit. Their story was that one of Arne's male cousins had been living in Germany with his German-Jewish wife and their daughter, Hanne. When the Jews were rounded up, Hanne was spirited away to safety by friends. It was close enough to be believable, and it accounted for her surname—Smit. Elsa's neighbors were kind to Hanne and helped protect her.

Though Hanne and Trudi felt the tension of the war in the adults around them, they blocked it out, not only by learning languages but also with games and make-believe. They created their own pockets of peace amid the turmoil. And they waited for Ada and Eli. However, after eight weeks Elsa believed in her heart that Ada and Eli were lost forever. She brought the girls together and talked to them as if they were adults.

"Hanne, you have papers that say you are a Dutch citizen named Hanne Smit," Elsa said one evening as they sat in front of the warm fireplace. Trudi and I also have papers—Elsa and Trudi Smit—and we will be a family of three. It is time now for us to travel to Britain. In a short while it will no longer be safe here."

"But what about Mutti and Papi? We have to wait for them!"

Elsa took Hanne's hand. "My dear," she said, "if they were able to come, they would have been here by now. You girls know what has been happening in Germany."

Trudi whispered, "They're capturing Jews."

"That's right. Hanne, your father is Jewish, and he's been gone a long time now."

"But Mutti isn't Jewish!" Hanne cried.

"No, but she married one, and that's often reason enough for capture. Your parents sent you here because they wanted you to be safe, to grow up, and to have a full life. They counted on me to make that happen, and that's what I'm going to do."

"I understand, Tante Elsa," Hanne said, as tears rolled down her cheeks. "I promised Mutti I would do whatever it takes to survive, and …" Her voice caught on a sob. "And I will!" Even at that young age, Hanne was determined to remain strong in honor of her parents. But alone in her bed that night, she hugged her little stuffed dog and cried herself to sleep.

"But why can't we all stay here?" Trudi asked. "Why can't we stay home?"

Elsa paused to take a deep breath. *This is so difficult*, she thought. "Because … because there's talk that the Nazis plan to take our country, even though we're neutral."

Elsa and the girls left on April 26 for Ijmuiden on the coast of North Holland, and gained passage on a ship to England. Two weeks later—on May 10, 1940—Nazi Germany invaded the Netherlands. Within a few days Queen Wilhelmina and her family, and the Dutch government, went into exile in Britain.

Chapter 4

Corry, England—1940-1950

Once in England, Elsa, Trudi, and Hanne made their way to Corry, a country village northeast of London, where Elsa had friends who took them in. It had been prearranged that if the time ever came when they needed to escape Holland, they would be welcome. Luke and Molly Ashworth were a warmhearted, sociable couple whom Elsa and her late husband had met at a party in London during happier times. They had stayed in touch through letters and phone calls, and the Ashworths had traveled to Amsterdam for Arne Smit's memorial service.

Luke and Molly had no children, and their cottage was very small, only one bedroom. However, there was a detached garage in back, which had been converted to a comfortable bedroom with sitting area, in anticipation of just such a need.

"It's lovely!" Elsa exclaimed. "The children and I appreciate it so much. I don't know how I can ever repay you." They were all speaking English now.

"Don't even think abut it," Molly said. "We've been friends for too long to worry about such things."

"But it even has electricity!" Elsa said, noting the lamp on the side table.

"Luke ran the wires from the house, but I'm afraid he's no plumber."

"Spot on," Luke said, grinning. "Afraid you ladies will have to share the loo with us."

The girls giggled and climbed onto one of the small beds in their new room.

Molly laughed. "Don't worry, girls," she said. "There's a chamber pot under each bed for emergencies."

Hanne and Trudi giggled again.

~~~~~~

Children who were forcibly separated from their homes and families found a measure of comfort in going to school and meeting new friends. The daily routine was good for them. Molly knew this, and she arranged for Hanne and Trudi to attend the village school, about two miles from home. They would walk there and back each day. Since they had arrived at the beginning of May, there would be nearly three months of school before the summer holiday, which would last just six weeks. Schooling was very important in 1940s England, and the girls loved it. Both were very smart, outgoing, and determined to do well.

A few miles beyond the school was a USAAF base. The United States Army Air Force occupied several bases in eastern England, some shared with Britain's Royal Air Force and some that were solely theirs. Occasionally, a small group of American GIs would visit the school, bringing gum and candy to the children. They were always welcomed by the teacher and certainly by the children! Hanne and Trudi, who spoke proper British English, thought the GIs were wonderful people despite their funny American accents.

One day in late July the GIs visited again, this time to give the children a little party to celebrate the end of the school year. They were all outside on the lawn enjoying treats and playing catch or tag, generally having a great time. Two of the men stood just a short distance from where Hanne, Trudi, and their new friend Kate were sitting on the grass, sharing a fresh pack of chewing gum. Aside, one man spoke softly to the other. "I'm hearing rumors that the enemy will be escalating very soon."

The other man responded quickly—in basic German, so the "English" girls, if they'd heard, would not understand. "Not here, not now. This is a party. We must protect the ears of the little ones. *Einverstanden?*"

Hanne spoke up in rapid-fire German. "We don't need to be protected! We know what war is all about. And I know what *escalating* means. We just have to make the best of it."

The GI turned and looked down, into her big soulful eyes. "You speak German? But … I've talked with you before. Your English isn't accented. It's perfect!"

"*Mijn Nederlands is ook.*"

"… What was that?"

"Dutch. Actually, my Dutch isn't perfect yet, but I'm working on it." She smiled shyly. "I'm also learning French from Mrs. Ashworth, the lady we stay with. Soon I'll have it perfect too. I love languages!"

And that was how the little girl with sharp ears, a quick mind and winning smile first caught the attention of the American military.

~~~~~~

The summer holiday passed quietly for Hanne and Trudi, though tension was still in the air, everywhere. Adults talked openly about the war that was happening just a short distance away and did not try to shield the children. They wanted them to be aware and prepared. For the most part, the village children stayed close to their homes. And Hanne still cried herself to sleep many nights, mourning for her dear parents.

One evening, Luke said to the family, "The Germans are bombing France now. I loathe saying this, but I'm afraid Britain will be next."

"Will we have any warning?" Hanne asked.

Luke nodded. "An air raid alert is in place and will sound. When it does, we all need to be together, huddled in the basement. I've made it as safe there as I possibly can."

Hanne and Trudi started back to school on September 4. There, the teacher talked with them, reviewing where and how they would congregate in the event of an air raid. "Now then," the teacher concluded, "if you are outside when the alert sounds, and you are close to home, go home. If you are closer to the school, come to school. Any questions?" Not one hand was raised. Reality had settled in.

Three days later, as Hanne and Trudi walked to school, the alert sounded. The girls stopped still, looked at each other in fear, clasped hands, and ran home. It was September 7, 1940. The Blitz had begun.

As the planes flew overhead toward the towns of Ipswich and Norwich, the children could hear them and imagined their big silver bellies full of terrible bombs. The noise was horrible, so frightening! The sounds would echo in Hanne's head as she and the others huddled together in Luke and Molly's basement under mandatory "blackout." The bombings always happened at night and were especially bad on moonlit nights. Sometimes the ground shook, and one time the children could smell the fire from an incendiary that landed in the countryside. Fortunately, the little village of Corry was spared, including the village school. Less fortunate was the nearby town of Ipswich, which suffered much destruction.

The bombing of Britain continued for eight months, until May 10, 1941, including seventy-six consecutive days over London. Nevertheless, the British did not surrender, and the attacks did not seriously affect their wartime industries. Miraculously—yes, it was a *miracle*—St. Paul's Cathedral in the heart of London remained undamaged, standing tall.

When the girls were finally able to return to school, they found that some of the American GIs had left a special treat for the children. This time it was something even more coveted than gum or candy, simply because of the short supply available to them—a basket of delicious, mouth-watering oranges!

The Blitz was over, but the cleanup would take a long time. Neighbors pitched in to help neighbors, and each day after school Luke would drive his old, nearly worn-out auto, taking Molly, Elsa, Trudi and Hanne to the outskirts of Ipswich to contribute to the effort. He felt it was good for the whole family to see what had been done and to help undo it. As before, children were not shielded from the war or its destruction.

They saw many things that made them appreciate their own good fortune, even without going into the heart of Ipswich itself. Though houses were still standing, debris was everywhere. One large piece of timber had knocked a big hole in the wall of a cottage, revealing broken glassware and overturned furniture. Molly, Elsa, and the girls put the inside back in order, as much as was possible, while Luke and another man patched the hole in the wall.

On another day, they found a small child sitting on a doorstep, crying over a doll with its head blown off. Hanne approached the child.

"I'm really sorry about your doll," she said. Hanne put her hand on the child's shoulder and sat down beside her on the step. "What's your doll's name?" she asked.

"Mary." The little girl sniffled. "I named her after the Virgin Mary because I wanted her to grow up to be a good dolly." She sniffled again. "Now she's dead."

"Well then," Hanne said, suddenly feeling very grown up herself, "if she's named for the Virgin Mary, then her spirit must have gone to Heaven." (Hanne had recalled a lesson from Tante Elsa.) "She's alive in Heaven and doesn't need this body anymore. You can keep it to remember her, but you can also be happy for her in her new home with God."

"R-really?"

Hanne nodded. "What's your name?"

"Annie. It's short for Annelle."

"Oh, that's very pretty! Annie, why don't you find a special place to put Mary's body—this body that she doesn't need anymore—somewhere that you can see it whenever you want to. You can remember her as she was and smile, knowing that she's happy in Heaven."

Annie's eyes slowly brightened and a small smile appeared on her face. "I know just where I'll put her," Annie said. "There's a drawer in the table by my bed, and it's empty. I can put Mary in there with her own little blanket!"

"That's a great idea, Annie. Why don't you do it now. I have to leave, but I'll come back tomorrow to see how you and Mary are doing."

As the child went inside, Molly Ashworth stepped around the corner of the house. "That was a wonderful thing you did, Hanne!" She put a motherly arm around Hanne as they walked down the lane. "Are you sure you're only eight years old?"

Hanne grinned. "I'm almost nine," she said. Hanne not only felt grown up, she felt very good inside.

~~~~~

In May 1946, one year after the war ended, Elsa and Trudi returned to Amsterdam. They wanted to take Hanne (who was now fourteen years old) with them, but Hanne begged to remain in England with Luke and Molly Ashworth. It was the only home she had known since being separated from her parents six years earlier. She had grown attached to the Ashworths and the little village of Corry.

"Aunt Elsa," she cried, having long since given up the *Tante* address, "I love you and Trudi very much, and I will never forget all you have done for me; but I need to stay here where I feel at home." Tears ran down her cheeks. "I was only in Amsterdam for six weeks. Holland is foreign to me." She glanced at Luke and Molly. "The Ashworths said they would like to have me stay, that I am welcome here."

"I know, dear. They told me."

Molly and Luke again assured Elsa that they would treat Hanne as their own daughter, and Elsa knew they would. She pulled her niece close, held her, and stroked her hair. "Your mother would be proud of you, Hanne dear," she said, finally. "You have grown into a fine young lady."

And so it was with sadness they parted on the appointed day, promising to write letters and to visit one another when possible.

What Elsa, Trudi, and the Ashworths did *not* know, was that Hanne's teacher at the village school was a "talent spotter" for the Allies, and that Hanne Smit, born Heide Rosenthal, had been unofficially translating letters and documents for the Allies for the past year. Multilingual talents were in great demand.

True, Hanne was not "official," but she was fully aware of her role and knew that there would be more work ahead for her as she grew older. *Important* work. Never forgetting what the Nazis had done to her parents, she was determined to *become* official, to avenge their deaths by serving— fiercely and without remorse—the beloved Allies who had brought an end to the terrible war.

During the next three years, Hanne was evaluated for her potential. By then, she was fluent in French, as well as German, English and Dutch, and continued translating for the USAAF on a heightened scale. During this time she also perfected another of her gifts: She could make up stories and convince people they were true. Following her eighteenth birthday, she volunteered to work for the American CIA, formerly the OSS (Office of Strategic Services). Among other duties, she was asked to impersonate a British Royal Air Force officer's daughter at a gala in downtown London, where she would have to meet and impress people with her intelligence and knowledge of French, as well as using perfect British-accented English. It was a test, of course. She was accompanied by an actual RAF officer posing as her father, and Hanne passed the test brilliantly.

"It was easy to deceive people," she'd said afterward, "because they wanted to believe what I was telling them. They *wanted* it to be the truth."

Hanne was then recruited by the Agency, given a new name—Charlotte "Charley" Stowne—and began formal training. She was taught to lip-read, eavesdrop and memorize. She learned about codes and ciphers, how to pick a lock, how to forge signatures, how to lose someone who was following her, how to inflict pain without leaving evidence … and how to kill. She was ordered always to carry a weapon. Best defenses, she was told, were shooting, stabbing and slashing—in that order. Charley chose to carry a small, sharp, pointed knife. It was lightweight, unobtrusive and silent. Hers had a ridged finger grip and a soft leather sheath, which she could pin into her clothing. She had several, and always carried a spare in her pocket or purse. She also was given a suicide pill—a capsule filled with potassium cyanide powder—to be used if deemed necessary.

You see, the only recognized "crime" in her new world was to get caught.

Chapter 5

Macon and Meadow Bridge, Georgia—2002

The plan John Jackson had referred to, the plan that didn't require Hannah to *think*, wasn't a plan at all. Doc and Laura merely outlined what they expected her to look for and to do regarding her friend, Martin Wynn.

"And, Hannah," Doc said. "I repeat: Take your time. Do this right, because we need to be absolutely certain. If Wynn is what we suspect, there could be others like him nearby who may, or may not, be aware of one another. If that's the case, we need to uncover all of them."

That was enough to convince Hannah this "assignment" was a huge research blunder on someone's part. *Sleeper agents in and around Meadow Bridge? Including Martin? No way!* She couldn't deny that someone shot a bullet through her window, but she didn't argue with Doc. She would just do the job. And, yes, she would do it right!

They briefly discussed audio/video recording devices and offered Hannah a secure cell phone.

"The cell phone, yes," Hannah said, reaching for it. "Recording devices—*wires*—no. Since I am supposed to assume Martin is a sleeper, I also must assume he'd be alert to such devices. Not a good idea."

Then Laura foolishly suggested Hannah use Internet forums or email to increase and deepen her contact with Martin. "Because," Laura said, "people tend to lose their inhibitions on the Internet. He could easily slip."

"Not if he's the intelligent operative you claim him to be," Hannah replied. She'd never forget the posters that circulated in the 1940s. Luke had shown them to her and to Trudi, explaining their meaning: *Careless Talk Costs Lives* and *Indiscretion = Repercussion*. She still believed those words. "I'd be willing to bet that Martin doesn't even have an email account," she added. "I certainly don't. In my day we didn't have technology and databases and hackers to worry about. We used good old-fashioned foot-and-brain work." She lifted her chin. "I do have a personal computer and I know how to use it. But I don't *play* with the Internet. When you've been in bed with the enemy, that's a sure way to get the covers yanked off—no matter how careful you think you are."

To Hannah's satisfaction, Laura managed to look both chagrined and disgusted, pushing her glasses up on her nose. *The recording devices were probably her idea*, Hannah thought, stifling the impulse to finger-point.

A few minutes later, she pocketed the cell phone and left Doc's office, head held high. She walked quickly to her car, her heels clicking decisively on the paving. She was fueled by the anger within. Fueled also by something else, which she could not deny—excitement! Yes, she was suddenly *excited* to be back in the game, particularly since she was convinced there were no dangerous people in Meadow Bridge. *A few young thrill-seekers, no doubt; or at least one*, she reminded herself, thinking of the sniper. She was certain that she could free Martin Wynn of all suspicion.

She stopped at a grocery store on the way home. She wasn't much of a cook, never had the time or opportunity to learn, and had survived chiefly on canned, frozen, and take-out food. There was one dish, however, that she could prepare very well. During her early years as Hannah Rosse in Meadow Bridge, a friend had taught her how to make the best beef stew ever! Sadly, that friend had moved away. Hannah cherished the memory—and the recipe. *Tonight*, she thought, *I'll cook for Martin*. He'd only been in her home one other time, and that was just for a simple dessert and coffee. They'd always gone to a favorite local restaurant for meals. Actually, "Donnalee's" was the only *real* restaurant in Meadow Bridge. The others were a variety of fast-food places where Hannah hung out when she was alone.

At home, she finished putting the groceries away and was about to call Martin to invite him, when the phone rang.

"It's Friday," Martin said, his voice warm and friendly. "Want to go to Donnalee's with me tonight?" Donnalee's specialty was chicken—every kind of chicken dish imaginable, each superbly prepared. There were also a few "seafarer's" items on the menu, the opposite of seafood restaurants that offered token landlubber fare.

"I was planning to make beef stew for dinner here at my house. Does that appeal to you?"

"Are you kidding?" He sounded surprised and happy. "Of course it appeals to me!"

After Hannah made sure the house was in order and that a delicious aroma floated from the kitchen, she dressed for the evening in narrow black pants and a pink knit top that flattered her toned body. One look in the full-length mirror satisfied her that continuing work-outs at the gym since she retired had kept her in good shape. She was still firm and tough—inside and out!

Martin arrived promptly at 7:00 p.m., looking very handsome in tan chinos and navy polo shirt. His hair, originally black, was nicely salted with gray, and his eyes were the color of dark chocolate. His smile could light up a room. Hannah liked him very much. Well, maybe a little more than very much.

He gave her a quick friendly hug, then asked what he could do to help.

"Everything's ready," she replied. "If you'll take the rolls out of the oven, I'll dish up the stew and we can get started."

"You made rolls? I'm impressed!"

Hannah grinned. "Pillsbury's little dough boy made them—I just put them in the oven."

They carried the food into her pleasant dining room where a carafe of red wine awaited them. After clicking glasses, they began to eat and talk.

Hannah, with her mission in mind, had a reason for inviting Martin to her home rather than going to Donnalee's. The restaurant—any restaurant—had too many distractions: people talking, music playing, waiters interrupting. Being there with friends was always enjoyable, sometimes downright fun, but tonight she wanted only to listen carefully to Martin, to hear him talk. Of course she'd heard him talk many times over the past year, but she'd always listened to *what* he said, not *how* he said it.

Now she wanted to know if any trace of foreign accent lurked beneath his southern drawl. It would not be easy to detect—Hannah was certain her native German speech and her British pronunciation of English were both sufficiently hidden under her current persona. She had found it easy to blend into not only the dialect but also the culture of the Deep South. Early on, she'd spent time simply watching, noting what people wore, how they moved and gestured. She observed that Southerners, for the most part, are friendly and trusting, particularly in a small town. If Martin were, indeed, a spy-in-waiting, Meadow Bridge would be an ideal place to "sleep." Hadn't she, herself, chosen it for its obscurity? Hannah, of course, wasn't sleeping. She was officially *retired* and loved her little town very much.

"You have a lovely home, Hannah," Martin said, "and you look absolutely beautiful this evening." He smiled at her over his wine glass.

Hannah returned his smile. "It must be the wine," she said, "but thank you." She knew she was still attractive, had been quite pretty thirty years ago, maybe even twenty years ago. But, beautiful? Now? When she'd first moved to Meadow Bridge, one of her neighbors had remarked that she resembled the movie star, Janet Leigh. Immediately, she'd had her hair slightly darkened and cut into the short, shaggy "do" she'd worn ever since, so she would *not* resemble Ms. Leigh. Did not want to attract attention to herself.

This evening, she had dressed casually but carefully before dinner and realized as she did so, that the last few times she and Martin had been together she'd actually *tried* to look attractive. For him. Reluctantly, she pushed the thought aside.

"I have a question for you," he said suddenly. "Why do I have all this gray hair and you don't have even one strand of it?"

This time she laughed. "You haven't figured that out?" Carol, her hairdresser, had been keeping Hannah's hair the same shade of brown for the past thirty years.

"I did. I just wanted to tease you, to hear you laugh."

They talked and laughed about many things that evening. And Hannah listened. After dinner they moved to Hannah's modest living room and Martin pointed to a framed photo on the mantle, the same one Hannah had rescued from broken glass just two days before. After putting her living room back in order, she'd visited the local Walmart and purchased a new, inexpensive frame. She couldn't bear not having that photo on the mantle where she could see it, even for one day.

"I noticed it the last time I was here," he said. "Your parents?"

Hannah nodded, wishing she'd thought to put it away, just for tonight. Aunt Elsa had given it to her shortly after she'd arrived in Amsterdam as a child. *They looked so happy—Eli and Ada Rosenthal, her beloved Vater and Mutter, Papi and Mutti.* "It's all I have left of them," she replied. "They died many years ago. In Atlanta." She added the lie automatically.

"Are they buried there?" he asked.

"No, they were cremated." A true statement, but not in the sense it was offered. Hannah needed to direct the conversation away from herself. They'd never discussed personal things, either of them. Maybe it was time. "What about you, Martin? I know your wife passed away shortly after you moved to Meadow Bridge. That was, when? About three years ago?"

"Three and a half, actually."

"Do you have family nearby?"

"No. Afraid not. I was an only child, and Emily and I never had children."

"Nor I. I've often wished there were children and grandchildren in my life, but it wasn't to be."

"When did Mr. Rosse die?"

"… Mr. Rosse?"

"Your husband. How long has he been gone?"

"Oh! You mean David. His name was not Rosse. It was Spencer—David Spencer. I kept my maiden name when we married." *Another lie*, she thought as she said it. *My maiden name was Rosenthal*. Which was why she'd chosen Rosse as her permanent name—it was close to Rosenthal, as was Hannah to "Heide" and "Hanne." So she had chosen "Hannah Rosse," a good name for what she'd hoped she would become—a good person.

"Why?" Martin asked.

"What?"

"Why did you keep your maiden name?"

"Why not? I was fifty-seven years old when we married—my first and only marriage—and changing my name on official documents and credit cards seemed like too much hassle to me. As it turned out, we were only married four years before he died of cancer. So, to answer your first question, David passed away eight years ago." She gestured toward the small round table in the corner. "That's his picture, there," she said, softly.

"I'm sorry, Hannah."

She shook her head. "I have no regrets. They were the four best years of my life," she said, thinking, *And that's the truth*. To lighten the conversation, she moved toward the little spinet piano that sat against a side wall and pointed to the framed picture that hung above it. "You'll have to look closely at this one, Martin," she said. "I'm very proud of it."

He rose and joined her and inspected the large picture. Then he laughed. "It isn't a picture at all. It's a jigsaw puzzle!"

"Yes. I put it together myself, treated it with special puzzle glue, and had it framed. What do you think of it?"

"I think it's amazing! I didn't know that could be done—sticking a puzzle together and framing it. Besides, the puzzle itself is complicated." It was a helter-skelter arrangement of every musical instrument imaginable, from piano to harp to violins, horns, drums, guitars, even bagpipes! "Must have taken a long time to put together."

"About a month. I just left it on the dining room table and picked away at it, a little at a time. It was fun!"

He smiled and shook his head. "And I suppose you also play the piano?"

"I do. Do you?"

"Are you kidding? My musical ability is limited to singing the hymns in church, rather badly, as you know, having stood beside me."

"You're too hard on yourself, Martin." Hannah sat down on the bench and enjoyed playing an abridged version of "Clair de Lune," just for him. After arriving in Meadow Bridge, she had treated herself to weekly lessons from her next-door neighbor, Lois Brown, a retired piano teacher who, unfortunately, had passed away five years ago. Hannah had continued to practice and to set new goals for herself. Music had become a calming joy in her life.

When she finished playing, Martin sat beside her on the bench and offered a clumsy, rather awful rendition of "Chopsticks," which made them both laugh.

"Where did you learn that?" she asked.

"Where do you think? In a bar, of course! Many years ago."

Hannah and Martin had a wonderful time that evening. In fact, Hannah had to keep reminding herself to listen for Martin's speech patterns. So far, she'd heard nothing to indicate he was shielding a foreign language.

As he was leaving, he asked if she'd like to see a movie the next day. "Saturday matinee," he said. "Good time to go."

Hannah smiled. "Animated feature?" she asked, rolling her eyes.

"No way! It's a movie for grownups, starring Harrison Ford."

"Say no more! If I don't like the story, I'll just sit there and drool over Harrison Ford. That's enough for me!"

He laughed, shaking his head. "You're a bad girl, Hannah Rosse."

He had no idea.

Chapter 6

After Martin left, Hannah poured another glass of wine for herself and took it upstairs to her bedroom. She dressed for bed but knew she wouldn't go to sleep anytime soon; so she relaxed in the soft, comfortable bedside chair and let her mind wander.

Yes, she had been a "bad girl"—a very *good* bad girl. The Agency and its operatives weren't always pure, honest and aboveboard, but they had an honorable mission—to protect the United States of America and its citizens. Sometimes Hannah's (Charley Stowne's) assignments were absolute dirty work and made her *feel* dirty. However, as a colleague once reminded her, "We do dirty work for a clean cause, Charley. We have to expect to get dirty."

She'd felt especially dirty on those three occasions when she'd had to take a life. After the first time, a concerned fellow agent asked her how she felt about it. She recalled: *Initially, I was glad I had accomplished my mission, done my job. Then, almost immediately, I felt an important part of me had died. Strangely, after that I was okay. I knew that if I had to do it again, I could. And I did.* She'd quickly earned respect among her peers as a tough, ruthless, focused agent.

She'd also felt dirty when she used a pen that shot tear gas at an unsuspecting foreign agent whom she'd befriended with her talent for deception. A very nice man who, unfortunately, happened to be working for the wrong side. And again, when she'd planted an exploding candle as a distraction and two innocent people were injured.

But her most *memorable* dirty deed didn't make her feel dirty at all, just clever and self-satisfied. Among her special assignments during those years was the gathering of information on site, whether in neutral or enemy territory. On this particular occasion she'd been ordered to extract critical information from a foreign female operative who'd refused to talk. The woman was tough. Charley had her in a bedroom of a protected house in a neutral country, and two of Charley's fellow agents stood just outside the bedroom door. The woman's hands, arms, legs, and feet were bound, but she was not gagged.

After trying several of the usual techniques to make her open her mouth, none of which worked, Charley called for a sturdy chair-size box, industrial-strength tape … and something else—something she, herself, had prepared in anticipation of the current problem. When the items arrived, she and one of the other agents pushed her prisoner into the box and taped it shut, leaving a small opening in the top. Then Charley removed the perforated lid from the glass jar she'd prepared; and, through the opening in the box, she poured a dozen squirming cockroaches. The woman's scream was blood-curdling. After just five minutes of screaming at the roaches and cursing Charley, she agreed to talk! Even now, decades later, Hannah Rosse smiled at the memory.

Sometimes, though, unwelcome thoughts pushed their way into her mind at inopportune times. Like last Christmas at her Sunday School party, when she and the other ladies sat by the tree exchanging "white elephant" gifts. *Everything looks normal*, she'd thought then, looking around the room, listening to the joyful laughter and conversation. *But they don't know that I, their friend Hannah who baked and served the plum pudding, was taught to deceive and kill.* Those kinds of thoughts were, mercifully, infrequent now; nevertheless, they still intruded two or three times a year, reminding her of a life she would never completely forget. Nor did she really want to.

She'd worked hard; she'd been loyal, trustworthy, and dependable for twenty-two years. And she'd been rewarded with the CIA Career Intelligence Medal "for a cumulative record of service which reflects exceptional achievements that substantially contributed to the mission of the Agency." She was proud of what she had done, and why she had done it. The precious medal was hidden in a secret compartment in her bedroom. Also hidden there was a "Cricket" given to her by a soldier of the U.S. 101st Airborne Division. The Cricket was originally a clicker used by music conductors in the 1920s, but the 101st Airborne found that it made a great signaling device for paratroopers to find one another after landing in darkness. The soldier who gave it to Charley was a friend for a brief time, which was all the time she'd ever had for various friendships. The only other souvenir from her career—the pointed knife with the ridged finger grip—was always on her person.

In many ways her work was exciting. Just like in modern movies, she'd sometimes dressed all in black, slid down drainpipes, crawled through tunnels, and climbed over high walls. But the work also had its drawbacks. Her entire life, from the time she was a child in Germany, had been a jumble of joys and fears, highs and lows, never knowing what lay ahead. And, when she was with the Agency, never knowing what (or where) her next assignment would be. When she'd applied for retirement just after her fortieth birthday—and just after her most dangerous assignment ever—she was ready for structure and routine. *I'd spent much too long as an instrument of deception*, she thought. *It was time to retire.* Sometimes during those working years she forgot who she *really* was; she forgot Heide Rosenthal. And for that, she felt shame. *It was time to redeem and rebuild whatever was left that might be worthy of redemption.* Fortunately, undercover agents were treated well at retirement, given good aliases (Charley had chosen her own—Hannah Rosse) and full support for their cover.

Now, in the comfort of her bedroom, she took another sip of wine and recalled more pleasant memories, those of her late husband, David, and their deep love for each other. When she'd settled in Meadow Bridge as Hannah Rosse, she adapted quickly and got involved in the community. There was no desire to become a recluse—only to live a normal life. That normal life included everything she'd ever wanted ... except love. Until, finally, after sixteen years, David Spencer moved to Meadow Bridge and joined the book club Hannah attended regularly. She was then fifty-six years old; and he, a little older, was a retired architect who had accepted a part-time job as a consultant to a new contracting company. As a widower with no children and no binding roots, he'd considered the move an adventure.

David and Hannah found they had common interests beyond the book club and started going out together. She recalled the first time David kissed her. Her lips were cool and unresponsive from years of trusting no one. But she quickly relaxed and accepted his genuine love; and exactly one year later they were married in the little church they both attended. Regrettably, she was then beyond her child-bearing years. David was truly the love of her life—the *only* love of her life. Oh, she'd had lovers during her working years, but nothing permanent. Most of them were men she'd used in the line of duty. *Get the information we need, Charley, no matter how you have to do it!*

Since she'd wanted to start their marriage by being honest—well, *somewhat* honest—she told David an older man had taken advantage of her when she was in her twenties. Actually, it had been the other way around. She also told him she'd worked for the government many years before, leading him to assume she'd been a secretary within a sensitive department. Still, she'd sworn him to secrecy. Yes, life was normal then, as normal as could be, and Hannah had felt blessed.

She and David had enjoyed walking together, up and down the shady streets of Meadow Bridge and through the town's only park, always holding hands. Young people would smile at them and giggle, probably thinking they were a little old for that kind of behavior; but the happy couple always smiled back, perfectly at ease. Their friends told them they were "cute" together, which they took as a playful compliment. Hannah thought those friends were probably envious.

When David died after they'd been together just four short years, Hannah was sure her heart had died with him. But her friends stayed close to her and helped her deal with her loss, especially Barbara, June and Eloise from the food bank; Betty from the book club; Suzy Carlson, the neighbor who raised beautiful roses; and the ladies in Hannah's Sunday School class. They reminded her of all the good things she had done for her church and community and that she still had many good years ahead. As her friend, Eloise, had said, pulling her aside, "You are healthy and young in spirit, Hannah. You won't ever forget David, and you shouldn't, but you *can* move on!"

Now, as she finished her glass of wine, Hannah recalled those words. *Maybe that's possible*, she thought, cherishing Martin's special smile that seemed always to be just for her, their walks in the park and easy conversations, and the laughter they enjoyed together. She rose, slipped into bed and turned out the light. As she eased her head onto the pillow, she smiled in the darkness. ... *One is never too old for love.*

~~~~~~

After David died, Hannah was incredibly lonely. She grieved for several months. And then one night, as she had many times over the years, she curled up in her comfortable chair, dimmed the lamp, and thought about the folks she had known and loved decades before ... and had abandoned. That was her only regret in choosing the life of Charley Stowne—the loss of her friends and loved ones. But she never regretted the *reason* for her choice, which was to avenge the deaths of her beloved parents at the hands of the Nazis. She was glad she had joined the Allies. She was proud to have become an American citizen!

With David's death, the sense of loss had been painfully renewed—her parents, her school friends, Aunt Elsa, Trudi, Luke and Molly Ashworth. Not a day had gone by in all those years that she had not thought about all of them, especially as she closed her eyes each night. She'd often wondered if they were still alive. Had they ever thought about her? Aunt Elsa was no doubt gone now, and Luke and Molly, but what about Trudi? *Trudi is probably still alive,* she'd thought. *Oh, how I'd love to talk with Trudi, my cousin who was once my dearest friend!*

Hannah stewed over this for a couple of months following David's death and finally said aloud to herself, "Why not? I can do it! I can go to the Netherlands and find Trudi!"

So in the autumn of 1994, at age sixty-two and newly widowed, Hannah Rosse boarded a plane with a new set of identity papers and flew across the ocean. She told no one where she was going, not even her former minders, though it would be quick and easy for them to find her, if they wanted or needed to. They wouldn't care anyway; after all, she was *retired.* She was on her own now. To her neighbors in Meadow Bridge, she simply said she would be visiting friends for a few days.

Chapter 7

Amsterdam, the Netherlands—1994

During the long flight across the ocean, Hannah's thoughts and emotions moved up and down from high to low, like a cockeyed pendulum. *I can hardly wait to see Trudi! Will we recognize each other? My dearest friend ever—I loved her so much!* And in the next minute it was: *What if I can't find her? She probably has a married name. She may not even be alive!* Then tears of guilt started to form. *Will Trudi hate me for leaving without a word, without saying goodbye?*

Of course she won't hate me. Surely she'll understand why I left. ... Or, after all these years has she become a different kind of person? Can she be trusted?

Yes, Hannah's survival instincts had kicked in once again. There was no escaping her training. She wished she weren't so alone. She wished David were with her. It had been only seven months since his death, but to Hannah it was an eternity.

By the time the plane landed in Amsterdam, though, Hannah's attitude was again positive. She had a mission, one that meant a lot to her, and she intended to accomplish it. Her former colleagues could have (and probably would have) helped her locate Trudi; but Hannah didn't want to tell them where she was. This was private. This was her personal odyssey, hers alone.

So, she thought, *I'll start at the beginning. At the house on the canal, where Aunt Elsa and Trudi lived when they opened their arms and hearts to me.* Fortunately, Amsterdam had escaped the bombing—though not the personal devastation it had caused—and Elsa and Trudi had returned home in 1946, after the war. During the next three years, Hannah (Hanne) had gone there a few times with Luke and Molly Ashworth for visits. She also had exchanged many letters with Trudi before disappearing. And she never forgot the address.

Her last visit was in 1949. She had been seventeen then and was just a few months away from assuming her new identity, her new life. That day, when she'd said goodbye, she'd known she wouldn't see her aunt and cousin again for a very long time, if ever, but she gave no indication. *Had Trudi suspected?* They'd parted with the usual cheerfulness and talk of exchanging more letters.

Now, forty-five years later, Hannah approached the house with anxiety and uncertainty. Early memories flooded back: her eight-year-old self, trying to balance a new identity with the loss of her parents; missing her school friends in Germany; learning to speak Dutch, as Trudi learned German; and the day Aunt Elsa told them they must leave the Netherlands, that the Nazis were poised to invade. She had never thought of those invaders as the *German* army. No, they were the hated *Nazi* army.

Hannah looked up at the house, which was obviously occupied. The narrow, three-story structure was attached on both sides to similar houses. She remembered just three rooms on each floor—one large in front, two small in back with a bathroom. Elsa had used her top floor for storage. As with all of the attached houses on the canal, the front faced the street and the water beyond it, with spaces to secure boats, and the back opened into a garden area. In later years, Elsa grew tulips in the garden to cheer her up. Hannah was pleased to see that some trees and pretty shrubs now grew along the canal side of the street, and a few public benches had been added here and there. In the old days the sidewalk had been bare and the houses, even before the war, had needed painting.

"I'm trying to locate a friend who lived in this house several years ago," Hannah said (in Dutch) to the elderly woman who answered the door.

The woman's welcoming smile became a chuckle as she said, "My dear, it had to have been more than *several* years. My husband and I bought this house in 1959, after it had stood empty for a year. Next month we'll have been here thirty-five years!" She smiled again and indicated one of the public benches. "Would you like to sit with me for a minute? Perhaps I can help you." They crossed to a bench and, grateful, Hannah sat. The air was pleasantly cool and the street relatively quiet.

The woman was probably in her early eighties, and since Hannah was a "young" sixty-two, she was addressed as someone much younger. "What's your name, dear?" the lady asked. "I'm Mrs. Dircks."

Hannah smiled and replied as she had planned, "Hannah Ashworth."

"Ashworth! You must be English." Hannah nodded. "Well," Mrs. Dircks continued, "I speak basic English. May we try it together? I could use the practice."

Hannah's sincere smile brightened. "Yes, if you'd like to." And she slipped into perfect, British-accented English. "I last saw my friend in 1949, when she still lived here. I don't know when she moved or where she went. Her name is, or was, Trudi Smit."

"I assume Smit was her maiden name?"

Hannah nodded. "We were teenagers then, so she probably has a married name now. Do you know any Smits who might help me locate Trudi?"

Mrs. Dircks shook her head. "Not personally. But my neighbor, Mr. VanLith, was living next door when my husband and I moved in. He and Mrs. VanLith were the first to welcome us to the neighborhood! He's a widower now, bless his heart. He might have known your Trudi Smit." She looked at her watch. "He's not home now, but he will return in … yes, in exactly seventeen minutes!" She chuckled and looked at Hannah. "Yes, dear, I can set my watch by that man's habits," she said. "He walks to the park every day it doesn't rain, leaving his house at exactly the same time each day. He meets a couple of other older gentlemen at the gazebo, sits and chats for thirty minutes, then walks home. It's his exercise and his pleasure. He's a fine neighbor," she added with a smile. "Shall we wait for him?"

Hannah felt encouraged. "Yes, please!" she answered. "Your neighborhood is much prettier than I remembered from my last visit. Of course, the war had only been over for four years back then."

"Unlike Rotterdam, our city escaped the bombing, though many houses sheltering Jews were burned. People just patched up as best they could and went on with their lives. On the other side of the city our home—Mr. Dircks' and mine—was one of those completely destroyed. My cousin and her Jewish husband were staying with us at the time."

"Oh, no! What did you do?"

"Abe was taken to a concentration camp. Very sad. He was a good man. Mr. Dircks and I stayed with some of our family members for a few years, until the government started building houses for displaced people to live. We moved into a new flat in 1950 and stayed there until we bought this house nine years later. Mr. Dircks wanted to be near the water. As a child, he lived on the canal, and it holds good memories for him." She adjusted her position to be more comfortable. "As I said before, this house had been vacant for a full year, which made bargaining for the price much easier."

"I wonder why it was vacant …" Hannah's thoughts and emotions took a worrisome downswing.

Mrs. Dircks could only shrug.

~~~~~

Hannah liked Mr. VanLith immediately. She judged him to be in his late seventies or early eighties and very fit for his age.

"I walk every clear day," he said, after introductions had been made. "And when it rains, I walk up and down the stairs in my house. Got to take care of these bodies God gave us, we do." They were speaking Dutch now. Hannah had learned over the years that most people—unlike Mrs. Dircks—would speak more freely in their own language, even if they also spoke English.

The lady politely excused herself. "I really must go check on Mr. Dircks," she said. "I've enjoyed chatting with you, dear, and I hope my nice neighbor can help you find your friend. *Vaarwel!*"

They waved to her as she walked to her front door, disappearing inside. "Her husband is an invalid," the gentleman said to Hannah, shaking his head as he sat down next to her on the bench. "Very difficult situation for both of them." Then his face brightened. "She mentioned helping you find someone?"

"Yes, I hope you can, Mr. VanLith. My friend—"

He interrupted her. "Please call me Lars. 'Mr. VanLith' makes me feel old!"

Hannah laughed. "All right … Lars." Then she said, seriously, "My friend and her mother lived in Mrs. Dircks' house before the war and left for England just weeks ahead of the invasion. Afterward, they returned here, and I was hoping you might have known them. Their name was Smit. Elsa and Trudi Smit."

"Hmm. That was a long time ago," he said slowly. "Almost forty years since we bought our house." He was thinking, and Hannah waited quietly. "There were two women living there when my wife and I came in the summer of 1957," he said. "I believe you are right—their name was Smit." He glanced at Hannah, shaking his head. "We weren't very well acquainted; there wasn't time. Shortly after Betje and I got settled, the older woman passed away. Then, right after the first of the year—1958, it was—the younger one moved out. You say her name was Trudi?" Hannah nodded and he continued. "I can't say for sure that was her name. Too many years have passed. And then the house was empty until the Dirckses bought it. Guess my memory isn't as fit as my legs are."

"That's all right, Mr.— Excuse me, *Lars*," Hannah said with a little smile. "You've done your best." But she couldn't hide her disappointment.

"Now, I didn't say I couldn't help you; I just said my memory isn't very good. I do know someone who was acquainted with the younger woman back then, and if you'll wait here for a few minutes, I'll call her and see if she has some information for you." He stood. "Your name is Hannah?"

Her excitement returned. "Yes!"

"I'll be right back, Hannah."

He had pronounced her name Hah-na, the Dutch way, which in that language would be spelled ... *Hanne*.

~~~~~

She could not hold still, as she waited on the bench. While ten long minutes passed, she tapped her feet up and down on the sidewalk and watched the activity on the street. Bicycles! She had never seen so many busy bicycles in one city. Finally, Lars VanLith returned, and the look on his face was triumphant!

He handed her a slip of paper. "This is Trudi Janssen's phone number. She used to be Trudi Smit."

Hannah jumped off the bench and shook Lars VanLith's hand vigorously. "Oh, thank you, thank you! This means a lot to me!"

"The lady I called knew Trudi's married name; so, we looked up the phone number. I didn't mention your name, because I didn't want her to call Trudi and spoil your surprise."

"Thank you again!"

"Would you like to use my phone?"

Hannah hesitated … and he understood.

"There are some phone booths," he said, "just a short distance down the street. He indicated the direction. "I'm sure you'd like to have a private conversation. It's been a long time."

Hannah nodded, tears in her eyes. "A very long time."

Chapter 8

Amsterdam, the Netherlands—1994

Hannah walked several blocks until she found a sandwich shop. True, she was hungry, but more than that she needed time to think about what she would say to Trudi. When she had arrived at the airport, she'd changed her money at a kiosk and checked her only piece of luggage, a small carryon, into an airport locker before hailing a cab. In her previous life, traveling light was the rule. Sometimes she'd traveled with no luggage at all, only a large purse. Simple, adequate clothing could be purchased and discarded as necessary. She had several false identities and was always careful, took precautions. On this trip, she had not reserved a hotel room by phone, because she wanted to appear in person and pay with cash. But first she would find Trudi!

By the time she finished her sandwich and tea, she had decided that the best plan was no plan at all. So she set off to find a phone booth, preferably one in an area not crowded with people. She didn't want anyone rushing her by banging on the door.

After a ten-minute walk she found just what she was looking for, a booth close to, but not in, a quiet residential area. She dialed the number, and a woman answered.

"*Hallo.*"

Hannah knew instantly that this was *her* Trudi. "I … uh, I'm a very old friend of Trudi Smit," she said in English. "My name is … Hanne Ashworth."

There was silence on the other end. Then a gasp. "Hanne? ... Hanne, is that you?"

Tears formed and rolled down Hannah's cheeks as she replied in barely a whisper. "Yes, Trudi. It's me."

"Where are you? Are you in Amsterdam? I'll come and get you!"

Hannah, her heart nearly bursting, managed to name the intersecting streets.

"I can be there in twenty minutes!

"Trudi, wait!" Hannah took a deep breath. "If anyone asks, my name is Hanne Ashworth. ... Please!"

"No one is here with me, and I won't be seeing anyone. Oh, Hanne, this is wonderful! I have dreamed of this day for years! Stay right where you are!

~~~~~

Hannah (now Hanne) sat on the bench next to the phone booth; and, once again, tapped her feet up and down on the sidewalk. Then she stood. Then she sat. She was nervous, excited, anxious—all of those things—as she waited for Trudi.

When Trudi drove up, parked the car and jumped out, she literally *ran* into Hanne's welcoming arms. They hugged and cried and squealed—two women in their early sixties—like the school girls they once were, oblivious to the automobiles passing by.

"Come, Hanne, get into my auto quickly. We'll go to my house where it's quiet. Oh, this is a miracle! I still can't believe it!"

As they drove into the countryside, Hanne asked, tentatively, "Do you forgive me, Trudi?"

"Forgive? There is nothing to forgive. I'd already figured out why you disappeared, and I knew in my heart I was right. Mother knew it too. I only wish she were here to see this day. She passed away a long time ago, Hanne. Peacefully, in her sleep. She was happy, as much as she could be with memories of the war all around her. And the loss of her sister—both of your parents—and *you*, Hanne. She loved you very much." Hanne, formerly the more talkative one, was quiet. Her tears were a strange mixture of joy and sadness.

"Luke and Molly are gone too," Trudi said. "They both lived long lives, well into their eighties."

"And your husband?" Hanne managed to ask.

"Eduard died suddenly last year. Heart attack. You would have liked him. He was a wonderful, sweet man who moved us to the country just so I could have a smaller, cozier house. A quiet place, not as busy as the city.

"Children?"

Trudi simply moved her head slowly from side to side. "It wasn't to be."

"I understand. My work made it impossible for me to settle down and have children."

"Hanne, you look wonderful," Trudi said. "All healthy and strong, just like an athlete. And pretty, too."

Hanne smiled. "Thank you. And, Trudi, you are as lovely now as when I last saw you." Actually, Trudi had gained some weight, but she was still pretty in that sweet, Dutch way.

"Enough fibbing!" Trudi answered with laughter. She then turned into a driveway and stopped. "Here we are!"

She did, indeed, have a pretty little house and a lovely garden. "It isn't much," she said as they entered, "but we were happy here. And now that I'm alone," she added, "I have *decided* to be happy! That's what one must do, you know—*decide* to be happy. Otherwise, one just wastes away."

"I do know," Hanne answered, and she told her about David.

They were seated side-by-side on a comfortable sofa in Trudi's living room, sipping on cups of tea, recalling their childhood and teen years with Tante Elsa and the Ashworths in England. And as they talked with excitement, they switched back and forth between English and Dutch. They had not yet discussed the "lost" years.

Trudi said, "When you told us goodbye that last time, I knew. I knew we probably wouldn't see you again, ever. But I never gave up hope." She set her teacup on the little table beside the sofa. "Knowing how much you enjoyed the volunteer work you did for the Allies, I always assumed that some day you'd become one of them, working—how do they say it now? Under the covers?"

Hanne smiled but didn't reply.

"You were so good at languages, Hanne, much better than I was. And you truly liked doing all of that number work at school. I did it so I could pass my levels, but I didn't like it. I was more interested in cooking, gardening, crafts, sewing—all of which account for much of my happiness at this stage of my life." She took a deep breath. "So … was I right, Hanne? Were you working under the covers?"

Hanne's smile was broader this time. She put her cup on the table in front of her and nodded. "But you mustn't ever tell," she whispered.

"I have never mentioned my thoughts to anyone except Mother, and I never will! That's a promise I will keep until I die!"

Hanne knew that Trudi was telling the truth. She reached over and hugged her cousin, her dear friend. Finally, here was someone she trusted, in a place where she could be herself. Not Charley Stowne nor any of Charley's temporary aliases, not even Hannah Rosse. Just plain Hanne, who, once upon a time, was Heidi Rosenthal.

The next day Trudi took her to the airport to retrieve her carryon. "Why did you leave it there?" Trudi asked. "Why didn't you bring it here with you?"

"Because I had no idea where you lived, or even if you were still in Amsterdam. I thought I might be staying in hotels until I found you." Then Hanne explained how she'd located her through Mrs. Dircks and Lars VanLith.

"Oh, Hanne, you are wonderful! I am so glad you found me—that you *wanted* to find me!"

"I wanted to contact you long before this, Trudi, but I couldn't. I think now it will be safe, as long as I remain Hanne Ashworth while I'm here."

~~~~~

Hanne stayed with Trudi for ten days, the most relaxing time of her life, except for her four years with David. Trudi drove her around Amsterdam and the province of Holland, showing her the Netherlands she had not seen when she was there for six weeks as an eight-year-old, nor when she had visited again as a teenager. It was beautiful!

"Many things have changed," Trudi said. "When we were together here as children for those few weeks, Amsterdam was nice, but much more plain. Everyone here was aware of the war but always thought of it as 'somewhere else.' The Dutch people had been at peace for so long that they could not believe it might happen here. They hadn't been involved in a war since Napoleon, and simply didn't anticipate the danger."

"I remember when Luke and Molly and I came back to visit you and Aunt Elsa after the war, this was a very sad city. But you were fortunate that Amsterdam survived with only minimal damage."

Trudi nodded. "We were. The real damage was to the hearts of the people, and to their health. When mother and I returned in 1946, Amsterdam was still feeling the effects of the previous winter. They called it the 'Hunger Winter.' With supply routes cut off and fields in ruins, thousands of people—men, women and children—died from starvation and cold weather in just the first three months."

"I was still a teenager in England then," Hanne said. "On a happier note, I remember the summer of 1951 when the 'Festival of Britain' celebrated the spirit of the British people, for prevailing over ten years of agony and suffering."

"Yes! We celebrated prevailing here, too."

They talked of many things; and then one day toward the end of the visit, Trudi had some news for Hanne. "The news is both good and bad," she said. "I've been considering how to tell you."

"Just say it, Trudi. I'm a big girl now." Hanne smiled encouragingly.

"It's about the war. You know that in January of 1940 the Nazis chose Osweicim, Poland, as the site of their new concentration camp."

"Auschwitz. Yes."

"That was just three months before you and I left for England with my mother. Well, back in the 1960s I met a woman who survived Auschwitz."

"Yes? Go on, Trudi!"

"She knew your mother there."

Hanne's eyes grew wide. "What ... what did she say?"

"The bad news is that both of your parents died at Auschwitz, which we had suspected. The good news is that the lady had remembered something your mother said in her last days. I'm sure your mother, my Aunt Ada, would want you to know this."

Trudi took hold of Hanne's hand. "A few days before she was taken away, your mother had a smile on her face and said to her new friend, 'My daughter, Heidi, will live to be a healthy, happy adult. That is how I endure this dreadful place. Whatever happens now, I am ready to go.' That's what she said, Hanne."

As Hanne's tears turned to weeping, Trudi added, "The lady told me she never forgot those words, because they inspired her. And she was glad she could pass them on to me." Trudi put her arms around her cousin. "And I'm glad I could pass them on to you."

"Did she ... did she say how Mutti died?"

Trudi tightened her embrace. "Yes. Your mother was not shot or tortured, Hanne. She simply gave up life, and then her body was taken to the ovens with others. That was in December of 1944. She *almost* lived long enough to survive."

Chapter 9

Amsterdam, the Netherlands—1994-2000

Over the next six years, Hanne visited Trudi three more times. Those vacations gave her something to look forward to every two years. She had *family*, and being with family brought a sense of peace and belonging. She and Trudi once again grew as close as sisters, exchanging joys, sorrows, confidences—and even, as they had in childhood, clothes!

On her second visit (1996), Trudi wanted Hanne to do the driving for their shopping trip. "That way I can concentrate on the places we need to go and the list of things we need to get. I'll be the navigator," she said.

Hanne objected. "With all those crazy bicycles? I'd rather not be ducking and dodging them!" she exclaimed.

"I'm sure you'll catch on quickly," Trudi offered. "You've always had good reflexes."

"And you're willing to take that chance? Oh, no, Cousin. I'm through living dangerously!"

Trudi laughed and conceded defeat.

During that same visit, Hanne was surprised and pleased when Trudi insisted they make a permanent bedroom for her in Trudi's home.

"We'll decorate it however you like!" Trudi exclaimed. "And we'll put clothes in the closet just for you." Then she whispered, "I promise not to borrow them!" Hanne laughed, and Trudi continued, "You'll have everything here that you would ever need if you have to leave the States quickly. What do you say?"

"Yes! I say yes, and thank you!" Hanne hugged her cousin. She now had a second home—a *real* home with family. And Trudi's foresight was amazing, because there could very well come a time when Hannah Rosse would have to disappear, again.

They had a great time moving furniture, painting, and adding personal touches to Trudi's guest room, now Hanne's bedroom. The change was dramatic, from neutrals to colors. White walls turned to sky blue with white trim; furniture, which had been painted brown, became soft yellow; and the drab beige bedspread morphed into a colorful, flowered print!

When they were finished, Hanne asked, "Do you like the changes?" Her eyes were glowing. "This is your home, after all."

Trudi laughed. "I like the changes because you chose them, Hanne. *You* like the room this way, and I couldn't be happier!"

Hanne hesitated just slightly. "Would you still be happy if I bought a piano?"

"A piano! Hanne, do you know how to play a piano?" Trudi's eyes were bright with expectation.

And Hanne's eyes brightened too. "Yes, I do. Are you musical, Trudi? I can't believe we've never discussed music!"

"Well, I can't play a piano or any other instrument, but I do love to sing, and Eduard always complimented me and said I was very good. Of course, being my husband, he would have to say that!"

"Then I will get us a piano next time I visit, and we'll make music together."

"Oh, Hanne! I love you! What fun that will be!"

Hanne then decided that when she returned to Meadow Bridge, she would have half of her (Hannah Rosse's) financial property transferred to Amsterdam. *I'd like to visit more often*, she'd thought. *Maybe someday, when I'm truly old, I'll move here forever, to finish my life in this place.*

~~~~~

Hanne's return trip in 1998 was truly a *homecoming*, and she stayed a full month. Yes, she bought a piano and discovered that Trudi had a lovely, natural singing voice. They spent many happy hours singing songs they loved from the old days—Dutch songs, German songs, and English songs they'd learned during their teen years in Corry, England. Eventually, they graduated to harmony, with Trudi singing soprano and Hanne doing her best trying to sing alto.

~~~~~

On her last visit (in 2000) Trudi presented a plan. "Let's go to Ireland for a few days," she said, "maybe even for a week. I have a couple of favorite places I'd like to show you! Have you ever been there, Hanne?"

Hanne hesitated. "Well … yes. But only to Northern Ireland in 1969. My memories of that visit are not very pleasant, I'm sorry to say."

"Oh, Northern Ireland is a different country altogether, and those were bad times back then. Not as bad as *our* war, but bad enough," Trudi said.

Yes, it was bad enough, Hanne thought, *fighting over civil rights. The Battle of Bogside, rioting in the streets of Belfast, and meddling by subversive outside interests.* That was the third, and last, time she'd had to "eliminate" someone. It was exhilarating to complete such a task cleanly, efficiently, and successfully; but it also was the beginning of the end for her, personally. *All I wanted to do from that moment on was to get out, to retire, to live normally.*

But all she said to Trudi was, "Tell me what you have in mind."

"We'll only visit the Republic of Ireland, the largest and greenest part of that island."

Hanne smiled. "Forty shades of green?"

And Trudi laughed aloud. "Yes! You can try to count them!'

"Did you know that phrase was coined by an American singer, Johnny Cash?"

"Then you will love being there for sure!"

They did go, and they stayed a week, spending their nights in various Bed-and-Breakfast inns (B&Bs), wherever they happened to be.

First stop—The Rock of Cashel, seat of the ancient kings of Ireland and later turned over to the church. A well-preserved ruin, "The Rock" stood high above Cashel town, and Hanne strained to see if she could locate their B&B from that distance. She couldn't.

Trudi teased her. "I can see it." She pointed. "Right over there."

Hanne looked again, then said, "Liar!" The "girls" had a laughing good time!

Before venturing out to the wild, unspoiled Dingle Peninsula, Trudi filled the tank with petrol. "We don't want to get stuck out there," she said. "Other than lots of sheep, the only life is more tourists, and not very many of them. The others don't know what they're missing."

They saw patchwork fields outlined with low stone walls. "Those walls," Hanne said. "They seem to go everywhere and nowhere." She shuddered internally but kept her thoughts to herself. The walls reminded her of that *unpleasant experience* in Northern Ireland. Not lots of walls—just *one* wall … and one terrible memory.

They also visited Gallarus Oratory, a tiny chapel on the Dingle, then ended their day with a nice dinner in Dingle town—roasted chicken in apple-bacon sauce, mashed carrots, and fresh fruit with clotted cream.

The next two days were spent seeing the sights in and around Killarney and, of course, shopping!

"This is a great place to shop," Hanne said, fingering a lovely piece of Irish lace.

"I knew you'd like it! This is my favorite shopping town in all of Ireland."

Last of all, they visited the Kennedy homestead. "I thought you might like to see where your beloved late President had his beginnings," Trudi said.

Hanne appreciated her cousin's thoughtfulness and was truly moved when they visited the Kennedy family's humble farm. A member of the Kennedy family was there to greet them and take them around the property. A small room in one of the outbuildings housed family photos and memorabilia, and the young man showed them video footage of JFK's visit to the homestead in 1963, just a few months before he was assassinated.

"It's amazing," Hanne said, as they walked back to their rental car, "to realize that this quiet, lowly spot is where 'Camelot' all began." She brushed at a tear as she remembered the moment when she'd heard that President Kennedy had been shot. She'd been on a lonely, difficult mission, and the news was heartbreaking.

"Thank you, thank you, Trudi," she said softly. "This has been very special."

Chapter 10

Meadow Bridge, Georgia—2002

As much as Hannah loved going back to Holland and seeing Trudi, she had never wanted to return to Germany, to Bremen. There was nothing there for her now—no family or friends, and probably no home, at least not the home as she had known it. Bremen had been heavily bombed during the war. All of the changes, plus those last memories of her dear Mutti and Papi would be too much to bear.

Now, it was 2002 and time for her next biennial visit with Trudi. But Hannah Rosse could not travel there now, not with her job still unfinished. Not until she either freed or condemned Martin Wynn. A trip to Amsterdam at this time would be too risky. If Martin were guilty ... it could put Trudi in danger.

When Martin came to Meadow Bridge and was subsequently widowed, Hannah hadn't intended to develop feelings for him, other than friendship. And they shouldn't become more than casual friends now, at least not until she proved he was everything he claimed to be. More important, until she proved he was *not* a sleeper. Still, if she were going to observe him closely for the purpose of seeking evidence, *something* would have to develop between them. Deceitful? Maybe, just a little.

Hannah enjoyed the Harrison Ford movie on Saturday afternoon and also enjoyed simply being with Martin. It was then she realized that spying on someone she liked and respected was much more difficult than taking an impersonal aim at an enemy target. Back then, she just did whatever the job required. Had she ever been afraid? Of course. It would be stupid *not* to be afraid. But life in Meadow Bridge was different. She was relaxed and happy. Hannah Rosse trusted her friends; she *liked* them. And Hannah Rosse liked Martin Wynn. A lot.

After the movie, Martin suggested they walk through the park. "To walk off the popcorn!" he said, grinning.

Hannah hesitated, but just for a second. Her only visits to the park since David's death were lonely ones, evoking memories, happy and sad. Could she walk those same paths with Martin?

"Yes," she said, confidently. "Let's walk." She returned his smile and they set off for the park.

Both were dressed for a relaxing late afternoon in Georgia's warm weather—Martin in light-weight khakis and a white golf shirt; Hannah in pale green cotton pants with sandals and a patterned top.

"I assume you've been here many times," Martin said. "Do you have special paths you like to follow? A routine?"

"You lead the way."

She was startled for a moment when he took her hand, leading her toward the path on the left. But he released her hand as they began walking.

After a few minutes of commenting on the beauty of the flowers and greenery, they stopped to watch a couple of squirrels climb a tree. Martin asked, "Did you come here with David very often?"

"Yes. What makes you ask?"

"Your demeanor, your hesitation." He smiled. "I'm a very observant fellow."

"Yes, we came here often," Hannah replied easily. "And I am certain this was a favorite spot for you and Emily. Am I right?" she added, with a lopsided grin.

Martin nodded. "And we held hands as we walked. I realized you and David must have done the same, since you seemed reluctant when I took your hand earlier."

"So that's why you let go." Hannah smiled and reached out. Martin did likewise, and they resumed walking, hand-in-hand.

A very observant fellow, he'd said. *Too observant?* Hannah wondered. In the past, she would sometimes get the feeling that the person she was talking with—observing—was actually looking *her* over. It was an uncomfortable feeling all those years ago, and it was encroaching now. Was Martin checking up on her? Could he possibly have a hidden agenda? A sleeper's job, while waiting to be called up, is chiefly to gather information about people who could be recruited as spies; or, to recruit someone himself. Was that Martin's mission in Meadow Bridge? She couldn't imagine a place less likely to produce potential spies. Or was there a more sinister objective?

"Tell me about Emily, Martin," Hannah said. "How long were the two of you married?"

"Ten years to the day, ten very good years. She died on our anniversary."

"How sad for you! She must have been young. What happened?"

"Emily was fifty-two and perfectly healthy until a massive heart attack took her life." He slowed his pace as he talked. "We were shopping in Macon at the time, and even though medical help was quickly available, she died in the ambulance." He turned to look at Hannah. "We had a great marriage," he said. "I loved her very much."

From the look on his face and in his eyes, Hannah knew he was telling the truth, and that pleased her. "Forgive my curiosity," she said. "It's just that David and I had a wonderful marriage, and I was hoping you and Emily had also. I know I told you earlier that my four years with David were the best years of my life." She smiled. "That's true."

He returned her smile. "Well, you know what they say."

"No. What do they say?"

"A person who was happily in love before losing that love is more likely to find love a second time than a person whose match was unhappy."

Hannah's response was, "Hmmm."

Together they picked up their pace and walked forward.

When Martin took Hannah home from the park, she offered him lemonade and they relaxed on her front porch. Conversation was easy, revolving around their common interests—working out at the gym, volunteering at the food bank, church activities, and books and authors. As Martin rose to leave, he said, "I've had such a good time today, Hannah. I'd really like to see you more often, if you're willing."

She stood, a little surprised. "Are you sure, Martin?" she asked. "There's quite an age-gap between us."

"Age doesn't matter."

"But I'm ten years older than you. I know, because one day the women at the food bank were trying to guess your age. You overheard and flat-out told them what it was!"

He grinned. "I'm not shy. Hannah, the way you look, walk, talk, your personality—no one would guess your age in a million years! And, as I said, it doesn't matter. Not to me."

She put her hand on his arm and replied with a sincere smile, "In that case, yes, I'd like to spend more time with you. This has been a wonderful day!"

He leaned over and kissed her softly on the cheek. As he turned and started down the steps, he called over his shoulder, "Bye."

Hannah stood there until he drove away, her hand resting on the spot he had kissed.

Slowly and reluctantly, she went into the house and began considering the situation she was in. *Come back down to Earth, Hannah!* She was supposed to be poking holes in Martin's stories, not accepting everything at face value and enjoying every minute with him. She sighed. *Okay, let's do it.*

She knew from her own experience that fabricating a foreign identity was a simple matter. False identities (perhaps of a baby who had died) and documents—a legal-resident permit, enrollment at a college or university, or permanent employment—were all one needed. Membership in a church or a community organization would be a plus. Ideally, the sleeper would be single and fluent in several languages. Hannah was definitely not a sleeper agent, but she was beginning to feel like one. *"One last job," indeed!*

Martin had said he'd attended a small agricultural college in Georgia. He also was a member of the same church Hannah attended, and she'd heard he went to weekly Kiwanis meetings in nearby Perry. *Easy to check.* True, he was married when he arrived in Meadow Bridge, and his wife had died shortly afterward. One could argue that she wasn't his wife at all but a fellow sleeper, and that Martin had lied to Hannah about his "great" marriage. Maybe he'd been slipping something into her food, gradually killing her, whoever she was. Emily Wynn had said she was born in France, and she did speak English with a slight French accent.

A voice inside Hannah's head screamed, *No! Not possible! Martin is a gentle person. He's my friend, my very best male friend!* She wished with all her heart that she had not accepted this assignment. But she had. And she'd been ignoring the first and second rules of engagement: "Trust no one," and "Never personalize the target." She wasn't an amateur. She knew better.

She hadn't trusted Martin, or anyone else in Meadow Bridge, with knowledge of her former life; but she *had* trusted Martin and others with her friendship. As for personalizing the target: *This is all backwards. Martin is a long-time friend. This was personal before he was a target!*

As a first step, she'd been listening carefully to his speech patterns, listening for foreign indicators. So far, she had not detected any—not Russian, nor German, nor even French. Not one syllable! And that was what she clung to.

Chapter 11

Thursday was a busy day at the food bank. So many needy people. Martin and Hannah were among the volunteers who packed grocery bags and helped the recipients carry them out to waiting cars. There were about twenty workers on any given day, serving not only Meadow Bridge but all of the surrounding area. More than a thousand families received this aid once each month, and they were carefully screened before being entered into the database. The entire project was housed in an abandoned church, which seemed an appropriate use of the building. It was managed by volunteers, and supported by cash donations and local food drives.

Hannah loved the work. It made her feel wanted and needed, as if her life in retirement had purpose and worth. Too, she had good friends there. All of the Thursday "crew" were retired—Eloise had been a teacher; June a nurse; Paul, an auto mechanic; Bob, a fireman; Barbara, a dental assistant; Brad a jeweler. They all knew Hannah as a retired bookkeeper; and, if anyone had ever challenged her, she had the paperwork (forged and provided for her protection) to prove it. When Martin recently joined the food bank volunteers, he told them he'd been a farmer before retiring.

On this day, Hannah was working beside Eloise. "I know you were a teacher, Eloise," Hannah said, "but it's been so long since we talked about it that I don't remember what subject you taught." Actually, she did remember, but there was a reason for bringing it up.

Eloise chuckled. "The subject I taught was popular back in the day, but it isn't in the curriculum any more, not in most anyway. It was Home Economics."

"Home Ec! I remember now. I loved it when I was in school. What made you choose to teach it?"

"Oh, I was a farm girl. My parents and grandparents were all farmers, and I grew up planting and cooking and mending. I enjoyed it then, and I still do."

"Well, you have something in common with Martin Wynn over there." Hannah indicated the table across the room, where Martin and Paul were working. Martin looked up and gave the ladies a wave and a wink. "Martin was a farmer, too, you know."

Eloise smiled and lowered her voice. "I think he was more of a reaper than a sower, if you know what I mean."

"Didn't get his hands dirty?"

She shook her head. "Not much. We've talked about selling crops at farmers' markets in the past, but Martin doesn't have a whole lot to say about plowing and planting, other than melons. Probably didn't take to it as a boy. Didn't enjoy it like I did."

That was not the reassurance Hannah sought. Outside, she used her secure cell phone to call Doc's private number. "Check to see if Martin attended an agricultural college in Georgia," she said.

"We did. He did. Abraham Baldwin in Tifton."

"Then he must have come to the States when he was very young."

"He was in his forties when he enrolled in college, and he didn't finish. Left after two years."

Hannah's heart sank, but she was also angry. "If you already know everything, what do you want from me?"

"We want the kind of information that only you can get."

She hung up on him.

~~~~~

Hannah wished she'd never met Doc. She didn't like him. He was a smart aleck, not at all like the folks she'd worked with in the old days. She looked at her reflection in the mirror as she applied lipstick. *Of course,* she told herself, *I was young then too.* Standing back, she grinned at her image. *And maybe a bit smart-alecky myself!*

She lifted the soft bangs that slid across the left side of her forehead. The scar was still there (though always masked with makeup) from the time an enemy soldier had slashed at her with a pocket knife. Fortunately, she'd been faster. And she hadn't bothered with slashing—she'd stabbed him, quickly and efficiently. There were other scars on her body, old ones mostly faded now, from a couple of bullets and some shrapnel. The only person in her new life who'd seen them was David; and, if he ever wondered how a government "secretary" had acquired them, he never said. He loved and trusted her.

She sighed. Time off—that's what she needed—time off from this ridiculous, painful mission. Doc had said, "Take your time, Hannah. Do it right." Okay, she'd take her time, and she'd do it right. But since there wasn't any big hurry, she'd make spying on Martin secondary to their growing relationship. At least she would try. Because she believed in him.

She put the finishing touches on her short, straight, easy-care hair. This was Friday, the day after she'd hung up on Doc, and she and Martin were going to Donnalee's for dinner. Smiling to herself, she went out to the front porch a few minutes early and sat down to wait for him. Several cars passed by, and then an unfamiliar one drove up slowly and parked in front of the house. *Oh, no. Not another one!* Hannah automatically slipped her hand into her shoulder bag and wrapped her fingers around the desired object. After a few agonizing minutes, the driver stepped out and waved to her over the top of the car. Immediately, she released the knife and actually jumped to her feet. It was Martin!

"Where did you get this gorgeous car?" she cried, walking quickly toward it.

He came around to meet her. He was grinning. "What? This old thing?"

"Martin, this is a *classic*, from … when? The early 1960s?" She reached out and lovingly touched the beautiful turquoise and white automobile.

"It's a 1957 Chevy Bel Air, No-Post Coupe," he said proudly.

"It looks brand new! How long have you had it?"

"I bought it about two years ago. After Emily passed away, I decided to indulge my passion for old cars. This one caught my eye immediately, but it was in pretty bad shape. I sent it to a restoration shop and got it back eight months later. I've taken it into the country several times, but this is the first I've driven it in town."

It was clear to Hannah that he adored the car. It was a beauty. She looked up at him and responded sincerely, "This is very special, Martin."

He smiled, opened his arms to her, and drew her into a gentle embrace. "So are you, Hannah. So are you."

He opened the door for her, and she slid into the passenger seat. Tonight she was wearing a plum-colored dress with a flared skirt that hung just to the top of her knees. The bodice was fitted, and the three-quarter-length sleeves were loose and sheer. Very feminine. Martin looked especially elegant in a navy suit with white shirt and tie, and Hannah felt like a princess riding with the prince in his royal carriage. *Or would that be a queen with the king?* She giggled aloud, as Martin put the key in the ignition.

"What got you tickled?" he asked. She told him, and he replied, "Definitely queen and king!"

Donnalee's special that evening was "Cherry Chicken." It had a fruity sauce, not too sweet, and Bing cherries adorned the top. Absolutely scrumptious! That, plus a good Chardonnay and candles on the tables, made the evening more perfect than it already was.

They finished their entrees and declined dessert—the cherry sauce on the chicken had been enough "sweetness"—then lingered over their coffee.

"This little restaurant isn't fancy enough for live music," Martin said, "but the piped-in isn't bad."

"It's very good! Listen to those violins. They're playing the theme from *Somewhere in Time*, my favorite movie!" Hannah was clearly enjoying herself.

"I don't believe I've seen that one. Tell me about it."

"It's an oldie, early 1980s, Christopher Reeve and Jane Seymour. He travels back in time, looking for her, and they find love in the past. Very romantic."

Martin cocked his head to one side and smiled at her. "Seems to me that finding love in the present would be much better."

Hannah's heart did a flip-flop, but just then the waiter appeared at their table with the check, and the moment passed. Hannah couldn't decide if she was sorry or glad. Her life was getting complicated very quickly!

Driving home in that '57 Chevy was pure fun. Martin took some back roads just to show Hannah how well it handled. "If only this were a convertible!" he exclaimed as they cruised along.

"Oh, no! That would mess up my hair!" Hannah raked her fingers through her short hair, and messed it up royally, sending them both into laughter.

It was dark when they arrived at Hannah's house, no moonlight at all. And the porch was especially dark because she had purposely left the light off to discourage those pesky flying bugs. When Martin walked her to the door, she leaned slightly forward, hoping for another kiss on the cheek; but this time, possibly because of the darkness, he surprised her. He lifted her chin and kissed her lips. She hadn't been kissed on the lips since David died, eight years ago! … *It was nice.*

~~~~~

The next morning Suzy Carlson was across the street in her front yard as Hannah stepped out onto the porch.

"Hannah!" Suzy called, waving. "Come on over. Have a cup of coffee with me!"

Hannah didn't hesitate. She liked her neighbor very much, and they often got together over coffee at one house or the other. "Your roses are especially pretty this year," Hannah said as she approached.

"Good weather for them, though we could use a little rain right now." Suzy opened the front door. "Come on in. Coffee's ready."

They sat at the little table in the breakfast room, and Suzy offered chocolate chip cookies to go with the coffee.

"Just one," Hannah said. "We have to watch our figures."

"Yeah, I'm watching mine all right—watching it grow!"

They chatted for a few minutes, until Suzy's curiosity got the best of her. "Hannah, I have to ask. Who was driving that gorgeous old Chevy I saw you in last night?"

"Were you spying on me?" Hannah teased. Or *was* she teasing?

"Well, maybe a little." Suzy managed to look coy. "I first saw it driving away from your house earlier. It really caught my attention. Then I 'accidently' saw it return. But by then it was dark outside and I couldn't tell who walked you to the door."

Hannah laughed. "*Accidently,* huh? It was Martin."

"Martin Wynn? But he always drives that Mercedes." Suzy looked puzzled. "I thought you might have a new beau."

"Nope. Same one, and he's not a 'beau.' He's a *friend.* Just a plain, old, ordinary friend."

"Hmph. You'll never sell that story to me, Hannah Rosse. And there's nothing plain or ordinary about that man!"

Hannah took a bite of cookie and sipped her coffee. "Suzy, what's your opinion of Martin?"

"My opinion is, if he isn't your *beau*, he should be!"

"I'm serious. What do you really think of him?"

Suzy considered. "He's a nice guy, nice to everyone he meets; he's good looking; he's involved in the community; he seems not to worry about money. I can't think of any negatives, not one. And both of you have been alone for far too long. You and Martin are good together." She poured more coffee into Hannah's cup. "I should be so lucky," she added.

Hannah recalled the day two years before, when Suzy's husband of nearly twenty years left her and their two young teenagers for another woman, shocking Suzy (and everyone else) to the core. She had not expected it. Hannah had stood by her, helped her get through the pain, and their friendship had grown. Now, she reached over and covered Suzy's hand with her own. "If you want it to happen, it will," she said. "Meadow Bridge may be a small town, but it has more than its share of very nice, available men."

Suzy smiled. "And *women*, unfortunately. I mean it, Hannah. Martin is a great catch for one of those women. Hey, if you don't reel him in … maybe I will!"

Chapter 12

That night it rained, as Suzy had hoped. By morning the rainfall had increased enough to be called a severe thunderstorm, and it was still coming down hard on Sunday. Hannah didn't feel like going to church and Sunday School, so she skipped, spending the day reading a humorous "caper" novel by one of her favorite authors, Donald E. Westlake.

She felt a little guilty whenever she skipped church, but sometimes—like today—she needed quiet time for herself. *At least*, she told herself, *attending services isn't a firm commitment like teaching Sunday school or being a member of the choir.*

When Hannah first moved to Meadow Bridge and began attending church, she was encouraged to join the choir. She had always loved music but didn't consider herself knowledgeable enough for the group. So she politely declined. However, several years later, after she'd learned to play the piano quite well, she decided to give it a try. Her voice wasn't exceptional, but because she could read music and stay on pitch, she was a good choir member. She stayed with it for two years and then gave it up.

There were two reasons for quitting. One was the commitment, not only to Sunday services but also to weekly rehearsals. She'd always taken a firm stand on commitment. If she committed to something—anything—she would honor that commitment to the end. Perhaps that stance had originated in her childhood, when she'd committed—with her mother—to her own survival. With the church choir, however, she found she could not always attend rehearsals and services. Life sometimes got in the way. Better to quit than have the group depend on someone who wasn't always present. Since then, she had been asked several times to substitute if someone was missing from her section. This she did, willingly.

The other reason for giving it up was Rachel Krenshaw, who sat next to her in the soprano section. Rachel was a busybody and a nuisance, always asking questions. Where did you come from? What did you do for a living? Do you have brothers and sisters? And a simple answer was never enough. Before and after choir rehearsals, and during breaks, Rachel tried to monopolize Hannah's attention. She also was one of the neighbors who walked every day; and, if Hannah were sitting on the front porch, she never failed to stop and talk, and talk. And talk! The woman wore her out. On those days, Rachel's favorite subject was politics. Hannah tried to appease her, but politics was one subject Hannah Rosse needed to avoid.

On Monday, rain continued to fall, but the worst of it had passed. She decided to call Eloise. There was a reason other than lunch. "Does this weather bother you? Want to meet me at Arby's for a sandwich? I need to get out for a while."

"No to the weather; yes to the sandwich! What time?"

"A half-hour from now?"

"I'll be there!"

They chose a quiet corner and settled in with roast beef sandwiches and drinks. As it turned out, Hannah didn't have to raise the subject she wanted to discuss.

"How are you and Martin getting along these days?" Eloise asked.

"What do you mean?"

"You've been seen together at several places other than the food bank and the book club. What's going on?"

Hannah pretended indifference. This was why she'd asked Eloise to lunch—to get an unbiased opinion of Martin.

Eloise would never hold back. She'd tell it exactly as she saw it.

"I'm not sure anything's 'going on.' We're just good friends," Hannah said. "What do you think of him anyway? In case I might, say, get more interested."

Eloise chuckled. "He's good-looking!"

"Come on, talk to me." Hannah smiled shyly.

"I like him. Martin Wynn is a good person. He's friendly, nice to be around." She sighed and spoke more softly. "Actually, he's a lot like your David was. ... I hope you don't wait as long this time. Hannah, if you don't mind my asking, why did you wait so long to get married? You told me you hadn't been married before David, and you were in your late fifties then. So, why? You're an attractive woman with a great personality, and you must have been even more so when you were younger."

Hannah, of course, had a stock answer for that question. She couldn't tell Eloise that the work she did for so many years wasn't conducive to marriage, commitment, or even love. So she said, "The right man just never came along. I was probably too fussy, but as it turned out, I'm glad I waited. David was worth it."

Eloise smiled at her friend. "I understand, I think. The old song says, 'A good man is hard to find.' Don't wait too long this time, Hannah. Martin *is* a good man." Then she raised an eyebrow and added, "Can't say I particularly care for some of his friends though."

"What friends?"

"You know. That creepy Art Lansfeldt in our book club. If he's not talking with Martin, he looks like he's out in a fog somewhere. Know what I mean?" Hannah nodded. "And Paul Smith at the food bank," Eloise continued. "Paul seems like a friendly enough guy, but there's something about him. ... He's just *different* from the other men who volunteer there."

"Hmm. Now that you mention it, yes. It's his personality."

"He tries a little too hard to be funny and ends up dropping verbal bombs, usually crude ones. Me, I volunteer there as much for the pleasure of being with friends as for the good work we do! I can't imagine Martin taking pleasure in Paul's company. Say, are you interested in seeing a movie tonight? *The Time Machine* is still playing at the theater and I've been wanting to see it. That sci-fi stuff fascinates me."

"Yes, let's do it!"

Hannah didn't care for sci-fi, but she did care for her friend. She had known Eloise for nearly all of the years she'd lived in Meadow Bridge. Not only were they both food bank volunteers and book club members, they also shared an interest in music. Hannah had encouraged Eloise to take her flute—left over from college days—out from the back of her closet and begin playing again. That was several years ago; and since then, they'd spent many happy afternoons together playing duets, Eloise on flute and Hannah on piano. They'd become great friends, even confidantes. Though Hannah's contributions were all part of her cover story, she felt she was good for Eloise in giving her a "sounding board," a place to vent. And, yes, the lady needed to vent once in a while—she had a short fuse and a problem with being patient! Lack of patience. That's why Eloise kicked her husband out of the house twenty years ago and declared herself a "free spirit" forevermore.

"Thank you, Hannah," Eloise had said many times, "for letting me blow off steam in a safe place. It keeps me out of trouble!" Eloise also had expressed gratitude to her friend for bringing music back into her life. Hannah cherished their friendship. And again, she felt blessed. *How could there possibly be spies hiding in Meadow Bridge?*

The rest of the week progressed normally. She didn't see Martin except briefly at the food bank on Thursday. But shortly before noon on Saturday, he appeared at her front door, still wearing his golf clothes. He played every Saturday morning, early tee time. "Care to go somewhere on the spur of the moment?" he asked as she opened the door. He looked tanned, fit, and healthy.

She laughed. "Guess you haven't heard my motto: 'Never turn down an invitation!'"

"Okay then, come on!" He turned toward the steps.

"Like this?" she called, pointing to her jeans and her Atlanta Falcons T-shirt.

"You're beautiful! C'mon."

So she went back inside, grabbed her small shoulder bag, locked the door, and quickly followed him down the steps to his "regular" car—a very nice, older model Mercedes.

"Where are we going?"

"You'll see when we get there."

A few minutes later he parked the car in the lot at ... Taco Bell.

She giggled and said, tongue-in-cheek, "Wow, this is special."

He replied in like manner, "And this is just our first stop. We're going inside and eat tacos with our fingers and make a big mess of ourselves." He grinned. "Now *that's* special!"

And they did. Well, they didn't make a mess, but they thoroughly enjoyed their tacos. There was no serious conversation, just talking and laughing about everyday things—dumb shows on television, card games, bungee jumping.

"Did you really bungee-jump, Martin?"

"Just once."

"Why didn't you do it again? Wasn't it fun?"

"Once was enough," he replied, laughing.

"I would *never* bungee-jump!" Hannah exclaimed.

"Never?" He took a last gulp of his drink. "You'd be surprised at the things you'd do if you're faced with a challenge." Quickly, he gathered the empty cups and wrappings from their table and stood. "Let's go, my dear. We have more stops to make."

"More? This is great—I love surprises!"

Their next stop was the park where they'd walked the previous Saturday afternoon.

"Didn't you get enough walking this morning around the golf course?" she asked.

He winked. "I rode!" He then took her hand and led her to a different path from the one they'd taken before. The weather was beautiful and their walk was truly delightful, maybe because they held hands the entire time.

If Hannah were honest with herself, she would acknowledge that she'd had a special interest in Martin for an entire year—long before John Jackson had stepped onto her front porch, long before Doc and Laura had poisoned her mind with suspicion. It was a year ago that Martin had begun sitting beside her in church. First, because he was a bit late, and there were few other seats available. But after that, he always arrived a little early and claimed his place beside Hannah. She liked it. His presence each Sunday lifted her spirits before the service even started!

At one point, she had considered taking golf lessons; but, no, that would be too obvious. Meantime, he asked her to have dinner with him—once, twice, again—and their friendship deepened. They'd been out together many more times than she'd implied to Doc. That's why the innuendo—*accusation*—against Martin had been so upsetting. Not only was it unbelievable to Hannah, it was hurtful.

Within the past few days Hannah's friends, Suzy and Eloise, had both offered their opinions of Martin. They liked him, they proclaimed him a good man, and each of them encouraged Hannah to make the most of her opportunity. In other words, as Suzy had shamelessly put it, to "reel him in!"

That was exactly what Hannah had intended to do, before Doc interrupted her life.

"Martin, did you say we have another stop to make today?" They were walking out of the park, toward the car.

"Yes, and I'm not saying another word about it." His smile was big, and he still held her hand.

"Three surprises in one day. What fun!" And she meant it.

Martin's third and final destination was a surprise in more ways than one.

Chapter 13

They left the park, Martin driving northwest out of Meadow Bridge.

"Where are we going next?" Hannah asked, quickly adding, "Never mind. I know what you'll say." And they both said it at once, "You'll see when we get there!"

They covered about twenty miles before Martin turned onto a much narrower paved road than the one they'd been on. Should she be afraid?

"I've never been out this way," Hannah said, making a mental map of their route. For future reference, of course. Again, old habits die hard.

"We're going for a drive in the country," Martin replied.

"Farm country, by the looks of it." She peered out the side window. "Not as many peach orchards here, like we have back home." The fields were planted with corn, soybeans, and crops Hannah didn't recognize. Peanuts, maybe? Tractors and other kinds of farm equipment were in evidence.

"Mmhmm. We've got a few more turns to make, and we'll be there."

"Where?"

"Oh, no, Hannah. I won't be tricked into telling," he said, teasing.

Two turns and a few miles later Martin announced that this was the final road before reaching their destination. It, too, was paved but just barely. Hannah slid her right hand to the clasp on her shoulder bag. Just in case.

"Looks more like a cow path than a road," she said. "A *pretty* cow path," she amended with a smile. And it was. In addition to the fields of corn and beans, leafy trees grew randomly alongside the road.

"It's county-maintained, and this particular road is not a priority item," Martin explained. Just then a beautiful old farmhouse came into view on their right. It was an inviting two-story with a wide front porch and rocking chairs. Good maintenance over the years was obvious. The lawn was pristine, shrubs pruned to just the right height, and azaleas in full bloom. Behind the house was a field of … something.

"What do they grow here, Martin?"

"Melons. Real good ones!"

"Watermelons?"

"Cantaloupe. Oh, here come my friends now. They've been expecting us." He turned into the driveway and parked. "I want you to meet them, Hannah. Come."

As they walked toward the attractive middle-aged couple, the woman hurried forward. "Martin! We are so glad you could come here today and bring your friend!" She spoke English with a distinct French accent, which Hannah noticed immediately.

Martin took Hannah's arm and introduced her.

"This is my very good friend, Hannah Rosse. Hannah, I'd like you to meet Jeffrey and Michelle Karroll."

The woman spoke first. "He means Jeff and Shelly! It's very nice to meet you, Hannah."

"I agree," said Jeff. "Welcome to our humble farm."

Hmm. No foreign accent from Jeff, Hannah observed. *Strictly southern English.* Both Karrolls were dressed in clean jeans and shirts, and Jeff had removed his baseball cap as they were introduced. Shelly's hair was long and dark and pulled back into a ponytail.

Martin and Hannah followed them into the house through the back door, which led to a spacious, updated kitchen. A homemade caramel cake sat on a lace doily in the center of the large round kitchen table, and places were set for four.

"Hope you haven't had dessert yet," Shelly said as she moved to fill glasses from a pitcher of iced tea.

"Too bad if they have," Jeff said to his wife. "They're gonna eat some o' this cake I made, even if I have to force 'em to."

"*You* made!" Shelly said, and Jeff winked.

"No forcing needed," Hannah assured them. "It looks delicious!"

"Is the tea sweetened, I hope?" Martin asked.

"Somewhat," Jeff replied. "Well, maybe more than somewhat."

Martin laughed and Shelly replied, "*Oui*, it's sweetened! What else would a good southern girl serve?"

Martin turned to Hannah. "I guess you can tell she's French."

Shelly joined the laughter. "Most obviously I am French, Hannah." She continued addressing Hannah. "*Cependant, j'ai epouse un garcon de ferme Americain, donc je parle Francais avec un accent du sud!*"

Hannah feigned confusion, looking first at Martin, then back at Shelly. "I'm sorry. I … uh, I don't understand French." Of course she'd understood it perfectly, and she felt a sudden knot in her stomach. *Is this a test?* she wondered.

"Oh, Shelly's just trying to be funny," Martin said. "She explained that since she married an American farm boy, she speaks French with a southern accent." His translation was correct.

"An' she's not doin' a very good job of it," Jeff drawled. "Shelly's been in this country twenty years, and she don't even speak *English* with the right sort o' accent. The way I do, o' course." He chuckled and gave his wife a hug. Jeff's accent wasn't just southern, it was *country* southern, Hannah observed.

As they sat around the table, she complimented them on their lovely home and the attractive property.

"This here house will be a hundred years old next spring," Jeff said, "an' we're thinkin' o' havin' a big birthday party for it!"

"*You* are thinking," Shelly corrected. "I am not having a thing to do with it. Too much work!"

"Hey, Shel, the food part's easy—just melons an' tea."

She shook her head in mock exasperation. Then Hannah asked how Jeff and Shelly had become acquainted with Martin.

Jeff spoke up, "Oh, he's been comin' here playin' in our melon patch off and on for 'bout eight years or so."

Shelly gave her husband a playful smack. "Oh, you! Hannah, Martin works hard when he's here."

"Off 'n on," Jeff added with another wink.

"But how did you *meet?*" Hannah persisted.

"We girls met first," Shelly offered. "I was in a long Walmart check-out line one day, and Emily stepped up behind me. I was holding a rather heavy box, and she asked me if I would like to rest it on her cart while we waited. I noticed the way she spoke, so I replied, gratefully, in French. We became friends immediately, and the rest is history. I was so sad when she passed away. Emily was a lovely person."

"Yes, she was," Hannah replied, "though I only knew her briefly."

"And now *you're* here, Hannah," Shelly said. "I hope we can be friends too. It's obvious that Martin thinks highly of you."

Hannah turned to Martin with a cocky grin. "Do you? Think highly of me?"

He returned the grin and drawled, "Off 'n on."

They enjoyed caramel cake and more light conversation, then Jeff proudly took his guests on a tour of their beautiful old farmhouse while Shelly tidied up the kitchen.

Inside, the house appeared to be just as well maintained as the outside. The rooms were large, the ceilings high, and the floors were hardwood. The furniture was old but, again, lovingly cared for.

"We added the ceiling fans," Jeff said, "to save on 'lectricity. But Shelly still uses the air conditioner. Overmuch, I think," he added, conspiratorially. But he was smiling and his tone was loving. It was clear to Hannah that Jeff adored his wife.

In the living room Hannah immediately noticed a gun cabinet next to the settee, but before she could comment, Jeff pointed to it and said, "You can see I like guns, 'specially old ones, like that there 1855 Springfield rifle-musket on the far end of the bottom row. It's my favorite."

"I don't know much about guns," Hannah lied, "but they look nice in this room. They go with the rustic décor."

Jeff laughed. "An' I don't know a thing about day-core!"

Actually, Hannah knew a lot about guns and recognized most of them, including a sawed-off shotgun—supposedly used only by police, military personnel and, unfortunately, criminals. Illegal for private citizens to own. *Hmmm.*

They made their way back to the kitchen, now all clean, where Shelly suggested a walk outside. "A short walk," she assured them. "To walk all around the farm would take an hour, at least."

"More like *two* hours," Jeff amended.

As they stepped onto the enclosed back porch, Hannah noticed something near the door. "Another gun, Jeff? Why isn't this one in the cabinet?" It was a 12-gauge shotgun.

"Oh, that's Shelly's varmit gun," he replied. "Got to keep it handy."

"… Varmit gun?"

"You know—snakes, and anything that goes after our melons—varmits!"

Hannah faked a laugh. Her internal alarm had been ringing since she'd seen the gun cabinet.

"You should see Shelly shootin' them varmits," Jeff continued. "Better'n any show on tee-vee!"

Guns, Hannah thought. *Plenty of them, including one at the door. And both Karrolls know how to shoot.*

"Come, see our melon patch, Hannah," Shelly said, holding the door open.

They walked across a lovely back yard and wandered around the front part of the melon patch. Hannah thought it was much too large to be called a patch; more like a small field. She had never been a farmer, even under one of her assumed identities, so she found the discussion of cantaloupes—growing, selling and eating—interesting. She also discovered that, despite her suspicions, she liked Jeff and Shelly Karroll, personally, very much.

"We four must get together again soon," Shelly said.

"But next time in Meadow Bridge," Martin offered. "Hannah and I will take you to our favorite little restaurant."

Hannah made a face and teased, "Taco Bell?"

He chuckled. "No. It's called Donnalee's, Shelly. You and Jeff will like it; I guarantee."

When they were ready to leave, the Karrolls presented each of them with a perfect melon.

"Oh, thank you!" Hannah exclaimed. She reached out and hugged Shelly with her one free hand. "Thank you for everything. It's been fun!"

As they drove away, Hannah said, "That was nice, Martin, meeting your friends. They have an interesting place there."

"Jeff and Shelly have been my friends for a long time. They're good people."

"Well, they certainly made me feel right at home."

"Good. Maybe we can visit more often and you can 'play' in their melon patch!"

Hannah laughed, then said, "So, Martin, I guess you speak French too."

He nodded. "Unlike Jeff, I had to learn in order to keep up with Emily. She insisted, and she taught me. I didn't really want to learn, but I'm glad I did. Do you speak another language, Hannah?"

"Sorry, not me," she lied. "The only language I speak is Southern! By the way, why didn't you drive the Chevy today?" Hannah needed to change the subject. "This would have been a perfect day to drive it in the country."

"Jeff likes to tinker with old cars. He would have had the hood up as soon as we got there, and I didn't want him messing with it. He did once, and once was enough. Besides," he added, "I was afraid that when we left Taco Bell you'd have sticky fingers and get taco sauce all over my fancy upholstery." Hannah poked him.

The sun was setting as they arrived at Hannah's house. She didn't invite him in. Truthfully, she was tired, and she could tell he was too. As he walked her to the door, she thanked him for a wonderful spur-of-the-moment day. "It was great fun, not knowing where we would go next," she said. "Thank you so much!"

It wasn't quite dark yet, but Martin didn't hesitate. He took her in his arms, tenderly kissed her, and held her close for several seconds. Hannah relaxed into the embrace, not caring if Suzy or anyone else was watching. As he slowly released her, he said, "I'm the one who should do the thanking. You're a miracle, Hannah. A miracle happening in my life."

As he walked down the steps, tears stung Hannah's eyes. She felt so *torn*.

Chapter 14

Despite Martin's warm kiss and loving words, Hannah couldn't shake the feeling that meeting Shelly and Jeff Karroll (especially Shelly) had been a test. It was the French that bothered her, that and the guns. Martin was fluent in French, as were Shelly and the late Emily Wynn. He'd even asked Hannah if *she* spoke a second language. Jeff was obviously a native of Georgia, French-speaker or not, but there was no doubt he could shoot. *Either Jeff or Shelly could have fired that shot through my window*, she thought. Were all three of them observing her? She did not like the thoughts she was having.

Hannah skipped church the next day to ponder her predicament. She knew she should feel guilty for missing church two weeks in a row, but the walls of her perfect world were closing in. Much as she hated it, Hannah knew she would have to give up the "time off" she'd so much enjoyed with Martin and give serious attention to the assignment she'd accepted. Her conscience would allow her to do no less, especially now that doubts were creeping into her personal space. *Never personalize the target!* Those words were cold and practical. They also stung.

When Martin phoned that afternoon to check on her, she told him she was going to stay in for a few days but that she would see him Thursday at the food bank.

"Are you sure you're okay, Hannah? Can I bring you anything?"

"No, I'm fine. I have several chores to do around the house, things I've neglected for too long. Washing curtains, cleaning rugs, boring stuff." They chatted for a few minutes, then ended their conversation with cheery goodbyes.

Hannah actually did do household chores during the next couple of days. She cleaned out a neglected closet, polished all of the furniture, and tackled her kitchen floor with vengeance. Rather than sapping her energy, the physical work *gave* her energy; and, by Tuesday evening she was eager to attend the book club's monthly meeting at the library. It would be a good opportunity to observe Martin's interactions with other people, as opposed to being alone with him. She hadn't paid much attention before, but then she hadn't been looking for trouble!

There was a small garden with a gazebo beside the library, and Hannah glanced that way as she walked toward the front door. The sun had set, but she recognized Martin sitting in the gazebo with his back to her. He was holding his head in his hands in a forlorn sort of way.

She was tempted to go to him but suddenly thought better of it. Instead, she moved quietly to the door and went inside. Martin had looked so vulnerable. Was he upset? Sad? Discouraged? Or was he feeling torn between loyalty and love—or at least the promise of it—as she was? Dare she hope?

Hannah had arrived early, and shortly thereafter her friends Betty and Eloise arrived and sat on either side of her at the conference table. Betty was Suzy Carlson's sister, and that's how Hannah had first become acquainted with her. Betty was often at Suzy's house across the street. Tonight the club members would be discussing Frank McCourt's middle-years memoir, *'Tis*, the story of his remarkable journey from impoverished immigrant to respected teacher and storyteller. Hannah loved this book and its message of perseverance and promise, and she was looking forward to the discussion.

Ten people were seated around the table talking with one another before the session began, and Martin had not yet joined them.

"So, where's Martin?" Betty asked quietly.

Hannah shrugged. "No idea."

"You two sure were having fun with your tacos the other day."

Hannah was surprised. "You saw us? Where were you?"

Betty grinned. "Not me. Suzy's teenagers gave me a full report!"

"Those little monkeys! I noticed them there with their friends, but I didn't realize they were paying attention to us!" Hannah couldn't help laughing.

"Are you and Martin becoming a couple, Hannah?"

"No, no. Not at all. We're just good friends."

Eloise had heard and interrupted, whispering, "Well, remember what I told you the other day. You *can* move on. It's been eight years, Hannah. It's okay."

Just then, the leader called the meeting to order and the discussion began.

Fifteen minutes later Martin came in with Art Lansfeldt, and Martin briefly apologized for both of them. Apparently, Martin had been waiting for Art in the gazebo, and Art was late. Hannah was aware that those two men always sat together at meetings. Martin joined in the discussions, and Art listened intently but rarely participated. If he had anything to say, it was usually limited to a handful of words. Until now, she hadn't given the pairing much thought. After all, she and Eloise and Betty always sat together too. Now, she recalled the first time she'd met Art, thinking he was a little strange, not very sociable. His physique didn't help. He was thin to the point of being skinny; and when he turned his head, it was with short, jerking movements that seemed to underscore his expressionless face. Hadn't Eloise referred to him as "creepy"?

As they were seated, Martin nodded to Hannah and gave her a puzzled look that said, *I thought you were too busy to be here tonight.* She simply shrugged and smiled.

After the meeting, Art monopolized Martin's attention as the group dispersed, ignoring everyone else, though Martin did wave to Hannah with an apologetic expression on his face. Hannah was concerned for him.

And her first impression of Art still hadn't changed. Art Lansfeldt was weird.

~~~~~

On Thursday after work, as the food bank volunteers walked to the parking lot, Martin caught up with her. "Would you like to have dinner with me tomorrow night?" he asked.

"Donnalee's, or Taco Bell?"

He laughed. "Neither. I want to take you to a special restaurant in Macon. I know how much you love music. This one has *live* music and offers more than chicken dishes. Want to go?"

The expression on his face was so ... so guileless, innocent, sweet. How could she keep up this charade? *Damn it! I want him to be innocent!* She'd learned many years ago that the enemy can be as close as a neighbor or friend. She just didn't want it to be Martin Wynn. She smiled brightly. "Yes, of course I want to go! Will we be dancing to that live music?"

"I do like to dance," he said, "but this place doesn't have a dance floor—just musicians. Sorry. Maybe in the next week or two I'll find us a place to dance!"

Hannah arrived home, tired and hungry. She made a tuna salad sandwich and took it to the little table on the front porch, along with a few chunks of fresh pineapple and iced tea. She had only eaten one bite of sandwich and one piece of pineapple when she saw Rachel Krenshaw at the end of the block, dressed in black spandex with a sweatband around her head. She was "fast-walking" her way toward Hannah.

Oh, no, Hannah thought. *Please don't stop to talk. I really want to be alone!*

As Rachel approached, she slowed her pace but didn't stop. Instead, she waved and called out, "I'll catch you on the way back, Hannah. Got to keep going just a few more minutes!" And she sped up again.

Hannah debated. Should she pick up her food and go inside? Should she eat fast and hope to finish before Rachel returned? Or, should she endure?

She chose to endure, because she really didn't want to hurt Rachel's feelings. It wasn't in her nature. She just hoped she could finish her meal in peace before the yakking began.

Actually she finished her sandwich and most of the pineapple.

"Whew!" Rachel exclaimed as she flopped onto the other chair. "It's a little warmer out today than I expected. I should have waited 'til this evening."

"You're keeping in real good shape, Rachel," Hannah observed.

"You mean for my age?" She laughed. "Exercise is the only way to keep feeling young."

"You're not old." Hannah took a bite of pineapple.

"I had a milestone birthday last week—number fifty!" she said proudly.

Frankly, Hannah thought Rachel looked every bit of fifty, but she gave her the expected gushy compliment.

"So how old are you, Hannah?"

Hannah put the last chunk of pineapple in her mouth and chewed slowly while trying to smile.

"Okay, I get it," Rachel said. "You don't want to tell. Well, I'm guessing we're about the same age, and I'll leave it at that!"

"Thanks," Hannah managed to say. She swallowed and pushed her empty dish aside. *You're off by a whole bunch of years*, she thought, *but that's just fine.*

"I do wish you'd come back to choir on a regular basis, Hannah. We need you. *I* need you to keep me on pitch."

"Sorry. I just can't commit to it—every Sunday, every Wednesday, and sometimes extra rehearsals."

"I understand, and I admire the way you value commitment! I'm only committed to a couple of things myself: the choir, my bridge club, and a little group of four—if you can call four a 'group'—three plus me, who meet once a month to discuss politics. We call ourselves 'Polo.' I think you would enjoy that, Hannah."

"No, no. I don't like talking politics."

"But you'd be such an asset! You're smart and quick-thinking. Our whole point is to try to make a difference, one person at a time."

"Thanks anyway, Rachel. It sounds like a noble cause, but I'm just not interested."

"Well, don't shut your mind to it entirely. Give it some thought." And then Rachel went on talking about the current administration, the Attorney General, the senator from Georgia, and even the mayor of Meadow Bridge! Hannah listened politely.

Finally, Hannah rose. "Sorry to break this up, Rachel, but I have chores to do before bedtime." She picked up her dishes. "I hope you have a nice evening," she added with a big smile.

"Likewise, Hannah." Rachel started down the steps. "And don't forget, you're invited to Polo. We call it 'playing polo!'" And she walked off with a spring in her step.

Hannah took her dishes inside, shut the door, and locked it. She looked at her watch. An hour and a half had passed since she'd taken her meal to the porch. *If I'd offered that woman iced tea, we'd be out there until morning! 'Playing polo,' indeed!* She shook her head. *Imagine going to "Polo" and listening to* four *of them yak politics at me!*

Then she had a sudden thought. *Politics, passion, fervor. What if Polo is a tiny group of subversives? A sleeper cell. Does Martin know about them? Was Rachel making noises to see if she could recruit me? That was part of a sleeper's job, after all. Will she try again? ... Or am I starting to see a serpent around every corner, serpents that don't exist?*

Chapter 15

The restaurant Martin had chosen for their special dinner in Macon was amazing and expensive. Hannah had never been there, and she was glad she had dressed for the occasion. Her "little black dress" and heels—not stilettos like younger women wore, but still fairly high—blended perfectly with the elegant atmosphere. The candlelit tables were inviting, the food was scrumptious, the décor soothing, and the live music came from a string quartet. The musicians were dressed in tuxedos and positioned in a decorative alcove. As Martin and Hannah were seated, the quartet moved seamlessly into "The Music of the Night" from *The Phantom of the Opera*.

"I love that beautiful song," Hannah said. "It has so much … emotion."

"Have you ever seen the stage production?" Martin asked.

"I wish! Have you seen it?"

He nodded. "Once, several years ago in New York. Michael Crawford was the Phantom."

"Oh, lucky you!"

"It's still playing, you know. Not with Michael Crawford, of course, but I'm sure it's still good."

Was he suggesting they might go to New York and see it? Hannah didn't comment. She merely smiled and turned her attention to the approaching waiter.

She had to admit, the whole evening—music, food, atmosphere—was very romantic! If only she hadn't had that niggling feeling of doubt. If only she hadn't had to remind herself it was a "working" dinner.

"Martin," she said, as their after-dinner drinks were served, "you've never talked much about your family, where you grew up, went to school. Tell me about your childhood." She knew that for a cover story to work, the details had to be mostly true. So when he said he was an active little boy, a practical joker, and loved sports, she had no trouble believing him. He even told a story about himself and his school friends. They had put wind-up alarm clocks in several hidden locations at his school and set them all to go off at the same time.

"We kids thought it was funny," he said, grinning, "but our principal had the last laugh. He pulled the fire alarm, which meant that everyone had to go outside. We waited out there in line until every last clock was located and confiscated. It was cold out, and we froze our asses off! Pardon my language."

Hannah laughed with him. "You said it was cold out. Where was it?"

"North Georgia," he said easily, "in the mountains. It gets cold up there in winter."

"I remember you said you were a farmer before retiring. I don't know much about farming. What grows in North Georgia? Tobacco?"

"We grew melons, just like Jeff and Shelly, but I didn't start farming until I was in my thirties. That was when I went to help my grandfather in Kentucky."

"Oh, where in Kentucky? I have friends in Lexington." It was a big enough city that Hannah could choose a random surname, if asked, and there would be no way to track it. She was a good liar.

But Martin didn't question her. Instead, he said, "Nowhere near Lex. Grandpa's farm was on the other side of the state, a few miles outside a tiny town I'll bet you've never heard of."

Hannah waited, expectantly.

Martin smiled. "It's called Monkey's Eyebrow."

Her mouth gaped open. "You're kidding me!"

"Scout's honor," he said raising one hand. "Monkey's Eyebrow, Kentucky."

Hannah couldn't help chuckling.

"Told you you'd never heard of it. Anyway," he continued, "Grandpa needed me. He had several acres of cantaloupe; well, he called them muskmelons, which they probably were, because Grandpa was always right!" He smiled and winked. "I stayed on and kept the farm going for a while after he died. Then I sold it and went off to college— an old man in a sea of youngsters. That's when I met Emily. Later, we became friends with Jeff and Shelly Karroll, and I started—as Jeff so eloquently put it—'playing' in their melon patch."

"Off and on," Hannah responded with a laugh.

Martin smiled. "What about you, Hannah? You said your parents died in Atlanta. Is that where you grew up?"

She shook her head. "No. We moved around a lot; spent most of my childhood in Alabama and my teenage years in Texas. That's where I learned to play softball and really enjoyed it, though I gave it up several years ago. Were you a baseball player, Martin?"

"Only for one season. I was a footballer in high school. After that, I fell in love with the game of golf. The golf course, as you know, is where I am almost every Saturday. Do you play golf, Hannah? Want to go with me sometime?"

"I'm afraid I don't know one golf club from another. I'd embarrass you."

He shook his head. "You'd never embarrass me." The look in his eyes made her heart melt. But what lay behind those eyes? Anything? Nothing? Or was he truly as sincere as he seemed?

They talked about other things, but Hannah could not forget something he'd said when discussing sports. He'd called himself a *footballer*, which is what soccer players are called in Europe where soccer is known as football. He'd slipped, and she hoped he hadn't realized it. He must have spent a lot of time there. When? Why? Had he been to Beaulieu in England—the secluded place for agents-in-training—before switching to the other side? That would make sense. *Frightening* sense.

But she didn't ask, not yet anyway. She had her own story to protect.

~~~~~

The next morning (Saturday) Hannah was once again sitting on her front porch with the customary lemonade. Martin, of course, would be playing golf. He and three other fellows were a regular foursome with a standing, early-morning tee time. Whenever he talked about golf, he smiled and his eyes sparkled. He seemed so normal.

Then she thought about their romantic dinner the night before, and the mixed feelings she'd had as it ended.

When he'd taken her home, she'd invited him inside.

"But only for a few minutes," he'd said. "All that good food and wine is weighing me down."

"You're not kidding me any, Martin Wynn. You're thinking about getting up early to be on the golf course!" She laughed; and he grinned, hanging his head in mock shame.

As he settled into the wing chair, his gaze traveled up to the mantle. "That picture of your parents, Hannah. It's missing."

"Oh. Yes, I, uh, moved it upstairs during my cleaning spree. Just changing things around a bit." She'd moved it purposely after Martin had remarked on it, because she was afraid he'd recognize her parents for what they were—a German and a Jew. Their features were obvious.

"I remember thinking that you look just like your mother," he said. "She was very beautiful."

Hannah was aware that even at age sixty-nine, she could still turn heads. But her reply was modest. "That's the third time you've referred to me as beautiful, Martin. I know better, but thank you anyway."

"It's true, believe me." He cleared his throat and furrowed his brow, as if trying to remember something. "Your father had a more exotic look. Was he from another country?"

At once, Hannah was on guard and very glad she had put the photo away. "No," she said. "He was an Alabama boy. A big fan of the Crimson Tide." That was probably the biggest lie she'd ever told. *Forgive me, Papi!*

"Did Alabama have a 'Crimson Tide' way back then?" he asked, smiling.

"Oh yes! That team has been the Crimson Tide since the early 1900s!" Hannah was no slacker. She'd done her research.

Now she was concerned that Martin might, indeed, be someone other than the person he had presented to the folks of Meadow Bridge. He had been fishing for information about Hannah's past, just as she had been looking for his. Why? Had she, too, made a slip of the tongue during one of their conversations? If he were really a sleeper agent, did she trigger an awakening? Did he suspect what she'd been?

Did he somehow find out that I, as Charley Stowne, was the one who killed a certain IRA terrorist mole—an important one, because he was a rebel with ties to Russia— in the late 1960s? Intel had confirmed that he was a bomb expert with big plans. Now she wondered if that were the reason Martin had come to Meadow Bridge in the first place. Had he been ordered to find her?

But that had been her job, and she had done it well! She'd been sent to Northern Ireland specifically for that purpose, crossing the Irish Sea on a smelly old fishing boat. It all happened such a long time ago, a lifetime ago. ... *Would it still matter to him?*

If so, the peaceful world she'd carefully constructed over the last thirty years could fall apart in an instant.

Chapter 16

She'd made it look like an accident. And no one had noticed, not until she was on the far edge of the crowd. Playing the part of a sweet Irish lass named Fiona, she'd joined a random group of revelers in a Northern Ireland pub one night, celebrating something. It didn't matter what. The Irish never need an excuse to celebrate!

She didn't know anyone there, but that didn't matter. This was the kind of celebration where everyone loved everyone else and no questions were asked. "Fitting in" was not a problem, especially for someone with Charley Stowne's talents. She'd been scouting her target for a few days, hoping for a situation such as this. It was perfect. Once inside the pub, she'd sidled up to him and started a conversation. He wasn't attractive. His nose was off center and the goatee did nothing to camouflage his nearly nonexistent chin. But she knew he was attracted to her, and she played to it.

As the evening wore on, the party grew, finally singing and dancing their way to the large terrace in back of the pub. Most of them were more than a little tipsy, and many were trying to step-dance (the Irish way) without falling down. "Fiona" was among them and had made sure she danced beside her target, bumping hips with him and batting her eyelashes. Within the surrounding crowd, it was easy to sing and dance toward the low stone wall enclosing the terrace, a wall purposely built to resemble the ancient walls scattered all over Ireland. She hadn't planned to do the job there—she had come only to observe him and make plans—but the opportunity was too good to pass up. With people all around, and the noise level extremely high, her well-placed foot tripped him as they smiled into each other's eyes and danced. Under the guise of catching him, helping him, and kissing him, she slammed his head into the stone wall. She knew he was dead on impact and she danced away, letting someone else discover him. She hadn't needed to use her trusty knife.

As she moved farther out, she heard people saying things like: "Ah, let the poor feller sleep it off"; "Can't hold 'is likker"; and "Sure 'n this is a real party!" Afterward, she disappeared, assumed another identity, and a few months later applied for retirement. The death was ruled an accident.

Yes, the death was ruled an accident. But had someone been there who suspected otherwise? Another terrorist? Had Martin been among the party-goers?

Again, she recalled Doc's admonition: "Take your time, Hannah. Do it right." What he'd meant was that her leads had to be solid, worth following up.

Okay. She would do it right, no matter how much it pained her. And it certainly was painful, because her emotions remained undeniably involved, even as her suspicions grew. If she turned him in and he was guilty, she would regret what might have been, and be ashamed because she'd been a fool. If she turned him in and he was innocent, her heart would break, because Martin would never trust her again. Aside from those few times when she'd felt "dirty" after completing an unpleasant, mandatory task, Hannah (as Charley) had never been emotional on the job. Now she was. This put her in an uncomfortable—and potentially dangerous—situation.

She began making notes: *1. Martin's comment about being observant, and his subsequent (correct) deductions during our walk in the park. 2. Entering agricultural college in his forties, and Eloise's perception that he wasn't much of a farmer. 3. The questionable visit with Jeff and Shelly Karroll. 4. His slip with the word "footballer." 5. The chummy relationship between him and the strange Art Lansfeldt. 6. His curiosity about the photo of my parents, and his particular interest in Papi's "exotic" look. Why is he probing my past?* It was a start.

She thought back to the time she first met Martin, when he and his wife, Emily, started attending church. The church folk had welcomed them with open arms, and they soon became friends with some of the other couples their age. Since Hannah was single—widowed—she didn't get to know them well, but she did sit across from them at pot-luck suppers a few times. They'd seemed like a nice couple—sociable, attractive, happy and healthy.

About a year later Emily died suddenly. There was no memorial service and no burial. Martin said that she had been firm about having "no fuss and bother, just cremation." The location for scattering the ashes was Martin's choice, and he kept it private. Hannah made another note: *7. Emily's quiet demise and inconspicuous, total removal from the earth!*

Another full year passed, and Martin had continued to attend church but only sporadically. Then one day he showed up at the gym where Hannah took an aerobics and weight-training class three mornings a week. She'd been going to that class regularly for several years, ever since David passed away. Not only was it a great way to stay in shape, it also provided a circle of friends that over the years had become important to her. Though the class was established for the "over-fifty crowd," that didn't mean it was *easy*. It was definitely not for wimps! Some of the younger members huffed and puffed their way through it.

When Martin had arrived for his orientation, he immediately spotted Hannah and seemed very happy to see a familiar face from church.

"Hannah!" he called. "How nice to see you!" He moved toward the treadmill where she was walking at a brisk pace. "You're covering a lot of distance on that thing. How long have you been coming here?"

"Oh, about eight years, I guess," she replied, continuing to walk. "Will you be joining our aerobics class? It starts in ten minutes."

"Don't know yet. I'm supposed to meet someone named Joe for orientation."

"I'm Joe," said a tall young man stepping up behind him. Martin Wynn?"

"Yes!" They shook hands.

"We'll be looking in on the class Hannah attends in a little while," Joe said. "You can see what they do and decide if you want to take part. Meantime, I'm going to show you our different kinds of exercise machines, the swimming pool, basketball court—lots of stuff."

"I know you'd enjoy our class, Martin," Hannah said, still walking on the treadmill. "We not only work hard, we have fun together!"

"Any men in your class?"

"Five out of twenty," she answered, grinning.

He smiled broadly. "Great odds!" *What a nice smile*, she thought. And Joe whisked him away.

Martin did attend class the following week and had been a regular member ever since.

Now, as Hannah considered Martin's participation at the gym more carefully, he had not begun as an out-of-shape man needing to improve his breathing or tone his muscles. He was in good shape, had great stamina, and only rarely spent time in the lounge area with "the boys," who loved to drink coffee and solve the world's problems. No, Martin Wynn wasn't there to *become* fit, but rather to maintain the high level of fitness he already possessed. He showed proficiency in aerobics class, moved smoothly and enthusiastically, and quickly caught on to new patterns of movement. He stood behind and slightly left of Hannah; and, as she watched him in the mirrored wall at the front of the class, she thought he would be a great contestant in a dance competition. He'd win, too!

Hannah smiled at the memory, then added another item to her list: *8. Physically fit. Years of specialized training?*

A week or so after that, he joined the food bank volunteers.

Hannah read through her list, then second-guessed herself. *I may be making way too much of this,* she thought. *Martin probably just wanted to meet people. His wife had died and he was lonely. Working-out and volunteering for a good cause are admirable things to do. Not only are they great ways to meet nice people, they give us goals and make us feel useful. ... Oh, damn it, Hannah! Get your act together! Get to work! Do your job!* Another item: *9. Volunteering at the food bank. An ulterior motive?*

So if Martin were really a sleeper agent, how long had he been in the States? He'd talked about that alarm-clock prank while in high school, somewhere in North Georgia where it was cold. Was that the truth? Or had he come here at the time he entered college? That would have been about fifteen years ago, if in his mid-forties at the time. Where had he lived after leaving college? He'd only been in Meadow Bridge about four years. *Must have been living in the South, because his accent is impeccable.* Hannah decided she would ask him, and then call Doc to find out if Martin was lying.

Chapter 17

Later that afternoon Martin phoned, saying that golf had worn him out, and he still had to cut the grass and weed the flower beds at home. "But I have an idea," he said. "May I pick you up for church in the morning? Afterward, we could have lunch together."

Hannah considered. "Hmm. I have a better idea. I'll pick *you* up for church and lunch. You've never ridden in my car."

She could hear the smile in his voice as he replied, "Are you a good driver?"

"As good as you are!"

He laughed. "It's a deal, but only if you'll let me buy lunch."

The next morning Hannah, dressed in a perfectly fitted, dark green pantsuit and floral-print blouse, drove her Nissan into the driveway of Martin's craftsman-style house to pick him up for church. She was curious to see if he really had stayed home yesterday afternoon to cut the grass, as he'd said he would. He had; or someone had. But the flowers still fought with myriad weeds. As he got into her car, she mentioned it.

"Oh, I was too tired to finish weeding," he said. "I'll catch up tomorrow."

Too tired? she wondered, as she backed the car out and drove down the street. *Or too busy doing something else? Like making phone calls, conducting business, connecting with his comrades.* She also began to wonder where his money was coming from. Did he receive enough on the sale of his grandfather's farm to fund his retirement? His home was very nice, and so was his lifestyle: *Weekly golf at the country club, which required a membership; membership at the gym; most of his meals in restaurants; a nice Mercedes in the garage; and an impeccable 1957 Chevy. The restoration of that car alone would have cost a quite a bundle!*

He interrupted her thoughts. "Aren't you afraid our church folk will think you're chasing after me?" he asked, grinning. "I mean, here you are, looking like a fashion model and picking me up in your car."

"Most of them have seen us together at Donnalee's more than once." She gave him an appreciative glance. "And you don't exactly resemble Leo the Loser, yourself. We're just spicing up the gossip!" She had to act natural, as if nothing were bothering her. But it *was* an act. And she was glad that acting was one talent she'd retained over the years.

They sat together in church, as they had the past several months, but not too close. Didn't want to add *that* much spice! And Anne Hargesty—new to Meadow Bridge—slipped into the pew on the other side of Martin, as *she* had been doing the last few Sundays. Martin's voice on the hymns was passable; at least he was in tune. And he paid close attention to the sermon, which at one point recognized the impression left by the often-heard responses, "My pleasure" and "No problem."

"Which response might Jesus have chosen," the minister asked, "when people thanked Him for feeding the multitude with five loaves and two fish? Would He have shrugged and said, 'No problem.' I don't think so."

As they walked to the parking lot after the service, Martin asked, "Where are you taking me for lunch?"

"I'm taking you, but don't forget you're paying the bill!"

"So where am I paying the bill?"

"Well, we don't have many options on Sundays in Meadow Bridge, just fast-food places. Chick-fil-A, where everyone says, 'My pleasure,' is closed." She smiled. "It really is nice, how they always do that. Anyway, we're going to one where they say, 'No problem.'" Martin chuckled and shook his head in surrender.

They had some pretty good burgers and fries, and then Hannah drove Martin home. When she stopped the car, he started to lean across the seat to kiss her, but Hannah stopped him. "Aren't you going to invite me in for dessert?" she asked.

He was momentarily taken aback. "What dessert?"

"Come on, Martin Wynn," she said, half teasing. "I know you always keep ice cream in the freezer. You've said so, more than once."

"Oh! ... Is ice cream good enough for a queenly fashion model?" he asked.

Hannah tilted her head without responding.

"Uh ... I guess it is." He climbed out of the car. "Follow me, your majesty." He seemed to have recovered nicely.

Hannah had never been inside Martin's house, not ever, and this was her entire reason for offering to drive him on this day.

~~~~~~

As she stepped inside, she could think of only one word to describe his home—charming. In a male-decorated way. The open floor plan, white walls, and mini-blinds on the windows gave it a light, airy, pleasant ambience, absolutely the opposite of what Hannah had expected to see. Actually she felt great relief. It was not the dark hidey-hole her recent suspicions had led her to expect.

"This is very nice, Martin! Simple and beautiful."

"I must confess, after Emily died I removed all of the drapes, doilies and knick-knacks, and had the tri-colored walls repainted."

"It suits you perfectly," she said.

"You like it?"

"I like it!"

He invited her to sit on the sofa while he scooped out the ice cream. The huge room had a living area with comfortable chairs and a TV, a dining area, and a kitchen area. From the sofa Hannah could, and did, watch Martin carefully as he took ice cream out of the freezer and scooped it into bowls.

"Chocolate or strawberry?" he asked.

"Any time chocolate is involved, there's no contest," she replied. "Make mine a double!"

Martin laughed and soon had ice cream for each of them. "I'm glad you like my favorite dessert," he said as he sat beside her. "I'll pass up cake, pie, pudding, cookies—anything at all, if ice cream is available."

"Me too, except I do enjoy a good cookie once in a while."

Hannah indicated the bookshelf across the room. "Looks like you have a nice collection, Martin. What kinds of books do you like to read, other than the ones we discuss at our book club meetings?"

He patted his mouth with a napkin and replied, wryly, "I don't always like the ones we discuss at book club, Hannah. I did like Frank McCourt's *'Tis*. And I liked that book Lee Iacocca wrote back in 1984, *Iacocca: An Autobiography*. I didn't get around to reading it back then, so I was glad it was on the club's reading list a couple of months ago."

"Speaking of our book club," she said, "I've noticed that you and Art Lansfeldt are good friends, but he rarely speaks to anyone else. Doesn't he like the rest of us, or is he just shy?"

"I don't think he likes or dislikes anyone, and he's not shy with me. But he is an odd duck, that's for sure."

"So, how did the two of you become friends?"

"I started it. I noticed he was always alone, so I introduced myself one night after the meeting. That was more than a year ago. I just thought he might like to have a friend. And, fortunately or unfortunately, he kind of latched on to me."

Hannah smiled. "You're a Good Samaritan, Martin."

Martin smiled shyly in return. "If you say so." He set his empty dish aside. "What kinds of books do you enjoy, Hannah?"

"I like to explore different themes and genres. But if I'm reading for escape—pure enjoyment—I prefer light mysteries with a bit of humor. Peter Lovesey, a British author, is one of my favorites in that genre."

"Which of his books do you like best?"

"I don't even have to think about that! I love *The False Inspector Dew*. It has a really wacky plot, is very satisfying, and was inspired by a true story. I've read it twice."

"Would I like it?"

"That's a difficult question." She considered it. "I really don't know."

Hannah finished her ice cream and walked over to the bookshelf. Martin's collection was eclectic—biographies, memoirs, general nonfiction and novels. Among them she noticed Johnny Cash's memoir, *Man in Black*; a two-volume (tattered) set of *The Outline of History* by H.G. Wells; *The Complete Short Stories of Mark Twain*; and an assortment of popular spy novels. She immediately recognized Daniel Silva's *The Unlikely Spy*, and an early edition of Somerset Maughm's *Ashenden*, because she, too, owned those books. She also owned John LeCarré's *The Spy Who Came in from the Cold*, which was not on Martin's shelves. But she kept those books and others like them upstairs in her bedroom, away from prying eyes.

Hannah was quite sure Martin didn't encourage visitors—he'd seemed reluctant to invite her in. And the open floor plan eliminated the need for her, or anyone else, to wander through the house. There was even a powder room opening off the living area.

As she turned back toward the sofa, she noticed a framed photograph on the end table. "That's a lovely photo of Emily," she said, returning to her seat.

He smiled. "Thank you. She was a good woman."

"Martin, you told me you met Emily while you were attending college. Where did you live after you were married, before you came to Meadow Bridge?"

"Not too far from where the Karrolls live out in Upson County," he said easily. "The nearest town of any size is Thomaston, which is probably why Emily and Shelly ran into each other at Walmart." He chuckled. "Only place to shop!"

"Did you have your own melon patch there?" She remembered Jeff's comment that Martin had "played" in his and Shelly's melons for about eight years.

He shook his head. "No. After I finished college, I realized that I wasn't much interested in general farming, so I earned a little money helping others take their crops to market, setting up, selling, things like that. Also, back when I sold Grandpa's farm, which was debt free, I could afford early retirement and that's just what Emily and I decided to do." *That answers the money question,* Hannah thought. "We settled in Upson County where we could enjoy the quiet life—reading, fishing, hiking. I liked bird-watching, and Emily loved flowers." He shifted his weight to face more toward Hannah. "We moved after a few years because the quiet life became *too* quiet. We needed—craved—a bit more activity. Meadow Bridge had a book club for me, a bridge group for Emily, and a church for both of us. It was a good choice."

Hannah smiled. "Yes, it was. I'm glad you moved here."

Martin placed a hand over one of hers. "I'm glad too, Hannah, especially now. I was lonely during those first couple of years after Emily died, but you have made these past months very special. I've told you before, I really care for you. And I mean it with all my heart." He leaned over and gave her a tender, gentle kiss, then put a finger to her lips. "Shh. You don't have to say anything, Hannah. I have a little surprise for you. Don't move." He stood, walked across the room, and opened a drawer in the sideboard, removing a small paper bag.

Hannah was bewildered and her body tensed, but she didn't move. Martin returned to his seat, holding the "surprise" close to his chest.

"I didn't plan to give it to you quite this way. I haven't even had a chance to wrap it. But the moment seems right."

She relaxed, because the look in his eyes was one of— dare she say ... love?

He handed her the bag. "Look inside, Hannah."

She peeked in, then reached in and removed an object wrapped in tissue paper. It was about the size of one of Martin's hands. Quickly, she discarded the paper and held a beautiful, round music box. The base was red, trimmed in gold and designed to resemble a curtained stage. Atop the stage was a small, ornate easel holding a little molded sign that read, *Phantom of the Opera.*

"Oh, I love it, Martin!" Hannah exclaimed. She immediately wound it and listened to "The Music of the Night." That's when tears came to her eyes. "This is the song the string quartet played at that special restaurant you took me to in Macon."

He nodded. "When I saw the box and heard the music, I had to buy it for you. I knew you'd like it, but I also had a selfish reason. Now, whenever you play it, you'll think of me."

How can I continue to doubt him? Hannah leaned over and put her head on his chest, where he held her in his arms for a long time.

~~~~~

She drove home more torn than ever. *Is he sincere? I hope so. Or is he simply a well-trained liar? He never said the word ... love.* She got very little sleep that night.

Chapter 18

At home, Hannah changed from church clothes into jeans and a T-shirt and settled into a good book. An hour or so later the phone rang. It was Betty, who was calling from across the street at Suzy's house.

"Hello, Hannah! Sis and I are sitting here twiddling our thumbs. Her teenagers are out with friends, and we're wondering what to do with ourselves. Want to come over?"

"And *twiddle* with you?"

"You got it!"

"I'll be right there."

Betty and Suzy were always good company, especially on a lonely Sunday afternoon, and something occurred to Hannah as she walked across the street—she could do a little "work" while she was there. Betty, unlike Hannah or Suzy, was an avid golfer. She and her husband were members of The Club. *Hmmm.*

"Welcome, friend!" Suzy said, ushering her in through the front door and straight to the den, which Suzy called the family room. Evidence of her family was everywhere—framed photos of her two children from babies to teenagers (none of which included her cheating ex-husband), a "young adult" (teen) novel on the coffee table, a debate trophy on the mantle, and a soccer ball in the corner.

"Hi, Betty," Hannah said, as she sat next to her on the sofa. "Are you going to teach my thumbs to twiddle?"

Betty laughed. "Now that you're here, we won't have to. We'll think of lots of things to do and talk about."

"But first," Suzy said, still standing, "Are we drinking tea or wine?"

"Silly question!" Betty answered.

And Hannah added, "Ditto!"

When Suzy returned with a plate of scones, three wine glasses, and a full carafe, Hannah looked at the spread and said, "Good thing I'll just have to walk across the street later! What about you, Betty? You live on the other side of town, and we won't have a designated driver."

"Not to worry. I'm spending a few nights in Suzy's guestroom. George flew to Dallas this morning on business, and he'll be gone three days. So, my friends, let's fill our glasses. Cheers!"

After the toast Suzy said, "Girls, I'm putting you on notice. I am *not* refilling the carafe when it's empty. There's just enough here to relax us a bit, not enough to get us drunk."

"Oh, poo!" Betty responded.

"Just kidding!" And their fun began.

They drank wine, ate scones, and talked about everything and nothing, even golf (thanks to Hannah). "How good are you, *really*?" she asked Betty, with a challenging smile on her face.

"Damn good! And I've got a couple of trophies to prove it."

"Are you always teamed with women, or do you and George play together?"

"On teams, I'm with women and George is with men. But we sometimes go by ourselves or with another couple just for fun. No competing allowed!"

"Do you ever see Martin on the golf course?" she asked, in a way that she thought was casual.

"Hah!" Suzy injected. "I knew you'd bring up his name, Hannah. Betty, did you know Hannah and Martin are 'seeing' each other, whatever that means?" Suzy was getting a little tipsy.

"Yes. Everyone knows that!"

"Everyone?" Hannah asked.

Betty rolled her eyes, then said, "Yes. And I've been at the club when he's been there. In fact, I've watched him play. He and George are in the same Saturday morning foursome, you know. I've followed them around the course a few times, cheering for George, naturally!"

"No, I didn't know they played together. Who else is in the foursome?" Other than mentioning their names once a long time ago—names Hannah had immediately forgotten—Martin never talked about his golf mates, only about the game he loved.

"Oh, let's see ..." Betty had to think. "Ron Hanson and ... Adam Calhoun—his wife's a bitch." Betty was getting tipsy too.

"I told Hannah to latch onto that Martin Wynn before someone else grabs him up," Suzy said. "Maybe even me!"

Betty turned to Hannah. "She's all talk. Pay no attention to her."

"I don't."

They all giggled, and Hannah decided to call it a day. "It's been fun," she said, heading out the door. She was tired and, yeah, a little light-headed herself. Maybe she'd go to bed early.

Now she had three more names for Doc to check: Ron Hanson, Adam Calhoun, and George Alcott. *Please don't let Betty's husband be involved!*

~~~~~

Hannah called Doc's private number the next morning, and he answered immediately. "What do you have? Do we need to meet?"

"Not yet," she said. "I have a question for you. Where did Martin live before moving to Meadow Bridge?"

"Farm country. Out in the boonies, a few miles from Thomaston, Georgia."

"Good. That's exactly what he told me." *He didn't lie,* she thought. *Maybe because he has nothing to hide!*

"Problem is, we don't know where he was before that. Prior to becoming an aging college student, Martin Wynn did not exist."

Hannah swallowed hard, then sighed into the phone. "Did you check Monkey's Eyebrow?"

"… What did you say?"

"Monkey's Eyebrow, Kentucky."

"Hannah, are you pulling my leg?"

"No. It's a real place. I checked. Martin said he lived there on his grandfather's melon farm for a few years, until his grandfather died. Then he sold the farm and went to college."

"I'll get back to you."

Hannah donned her work-out clothes and headed for the gym. If Doc's super-team could not verify the "grandfather's farm" story, then it was all but over. She would give up Jeff and Shelly Karroll, and then it would most *certainly* be over. When she'd met the Karrolls, she'd felt she was being tested. That business with speaking French—Shelly, Emily, Martin—what was that all about? And the guns. The whole set-up had aroused her suspicions. And she'd continued to make excuses for those suspicions. She had not done her job.

So, why did Martin and Emily Wynn *really* move to Meadow Bridge? If he were a sleeper, were there others living among Hannah's peaceful surroundings? Sleepers didn't generally associate with one another, or even *know* one another, but Doc had suggested that collusion was a real possibility in this case. Were some of her friends involved? Then she had a startling thought: *If Martin's golf buddies— including Betty's husband, George—are a team of sleepers, it's possible that Betty is involved too! What about Suzy?* Could Hannah trust *anybody*?

She avoided Martin during the next three days, though she did talk with him on the phone each day, briefly but nicely. She told him she was going shopping in Perry with Eloise on Monday (She did. It was enjoyable.); visiting friends in Fort Valley on Tuesday (Did not. She spent the day there in the library.) and, she awaited Doc's call in the privacy of her home.

Her phone rang late Wednesday afternoon. "No record of him in Monkey's Eyebrow—stupid name for a town!—at least not as Martin Wynn," Doc said. "The few farms that were there had been in the families for decades, none sold within the last five to fifteen years, and not a Wynn among them, though it could have been his maternal grandfather," he added grudgingly. So we sent a team door to door with his college photo. Also showed it to some old-timers around the area. Nothing. He fed you a load of shit, Hannah. ... Hannah? Are you still there?"

She had closed her eyes tightly against the implications. Recovering quickly, she answered, "Yes. I'm here." She composed herself and read him the list of her observations, item by item, withholding only one—the Karrolls—but stressing her uneasiness about Emily Wynn's disappearance. "Was there proof of her cremation?" Hannah asked.

"None. Probably still alive somewhere. She did have a U.S. passport and a birth certificate, no doubt forgeries. Naturalized citizen. Born in France to French parents."

"That's another thing," Hannah began. She had no choice now. It was time to tell Doc about Jeff and Shelly Karroll. So she filled him in on the afternoon she and Martin had spent at their farm, told him about the guns, and ended by saying, "Shelly Karroll is French, or at least she claims to be, and Martin is skilled in that language."

"Smoke screen. They're no doubt using it as a cover language to mask their origins. You've done the same thing, Hannah."

She didn't like being reminded. Doc was right. And she still didn't like him.

"There's something else I hope you're aware of, Hannah," Doc said. "It's possible that Wynn has been activated for only one reason—to get *you*."

Hannah's eyes grew wide. "But that's not ..."

"Yes it is. Consider some of the things you've accomplished over the years, particularly that Irish incident just before you retired. That one would not be easy for an enemy to forget. Yes, it's entirely possible you've been unmasked and are now a target. Be very careful!"

Careful of Martin? She held her breath.

"You've turned up some excellent leads," Doc continued, in an uncharacteristic softening tone, "especially this info on the Karrolls. We'll check them out immediately. And, Hannah, whatever method you're using to get close to Martin Wynn is working. Stay with it, because we need one more thing before we break this loose."

"Yes?"

"We need to know who else is sleeping in Meadow Bridge."

~~~~~~

It was dinner time, but Hannah wasn't hungry. There wasn't much in her refrigerator anyway. She pulled out a small container of fruit yogurt, and made a cup of herbal tea. Doc had said, "Whatever method you're using ..." But she hadn't been using a method to trap Martin. She honestly liked the man very much, and lately she even thought she might love him. Now, though, she had to face the truth. At the very least, Martin Wynn was a liar. *And I was an idiot*, she thought. She'd been fooling herself about Martin. So why was she shocked when she finally realized that she *had* been fooling herself? *Gullible, that's what I've been!* He was most probably a foreign agent who had been toying with her feelings; and, at the same time looking for proof that she was Charley Stowne, Killer in Hiding. So he could expose her. Or worse, "eliminate" her. That made her angry—actually, *mad*—and ignited the tough, no-nonsense, gritty attitude, the inner strength, and the resolve that had been so much a part of her for so many years.

She spent the evening in "Charley" mode—going over previous events and conversations in her head with fierce concentration, making more notes, planning, and deciding on the best course of action. She was smart, careful, and thorough. From this time forward, Hannah Rosse would have a method! *I'll get him,* she vowed. *I won't let him get me first!*

Finally, at nearly midnight she went upstairs and got ready for bed. With her head on the pillow, she reached over and turned off the lamp on her bedside stand; and, in the darkness, she picked up the little "Phantom" music box beside the lamp, stroking it gently with her fingers. She'd put it on the stand Sunday night after arriving home from Martin's. That night, she'd wound it up several times before happily falling asleep to "The Music of the Night." Now, she wound it up only once ... and wept. For the last time.

Chapter 19

Hannah slept a little longer the next morning, which made her about fifteen minutes late arriving at the food bank. As she entered the work area, Martin walked quickly toward her.

"Where have you been?" he asked in a lowered voice. "I've been worried about you. Is everything all right?"

Her false demeanor was bright and cheerful. "Just fine! I forgot to set my alarm and didn't wake up on time." She poked him playfully. "Have you been doing my work for me?"

He relaxed. "You kidding? I've got enough to do. Eloise may throw a fit, though. There's no one else to help her this morning. Barbara's out of town, and June had a massage appointment."

"Massage? Mmm. That sounds nice."

She saw Eloise motioning frantically for her to hurry. "Gotta run," Hanna said. "See you later!"

They worked hard that morning, not a lot of time for girl talk, which was probably a good thing. Hannah noted that Martin and Paul were working together as usual, as were Bob and Brad. They always paired off that way. The women, however, often mixed it up.

Bob the fireman and Brad the jeweler seemed to be good friends. They laughed a lot as they worked and were friendly with the rest of the crew too. Martin and Paul, the auto mechanic, also seemed to work well together. But Hannah recalled Eloise's comment about Paul's "dropping verbal bombs." Yes, Paul's sense of humor bordered on crude. Sometimes his remarks were downright embarrassing. Could Paul possibly be a sleeper agent? He sure didn't look or act like one. But that was the whole point, wasn't it? Back in the day, Hannah could get inside the heads of the persons she created. She *became* them. Is that what Paul "Smith" had done? He had that disgusting habit of scratching his crotch every few minutes. Was that faked, or did it really itch? Repulsive!

The food bank always closed at 1:00 p.m., but by the time the volunteers locked up and left, it was closer to 2:00. Hannah walked to the parking lot with Martin, as she'd been doing lately. Paul walked in the other direction, scratching.

"Want to get some lunch with me?" she asked. "I'll catch you up on my last few days of adventure." Her practiced tone was upbeat, encouraging.

"I'd begun to think you were avoiding me."

"Not a chance!" She slipped her arm in his. "Where shall we go?"

He grinned. "Taco Bell?"

"Sure. Why not."

"I'll drive," he said, walking her toward his car. "I need to make a quick stop on the way."

In a few minutes he pulled into a drugstore parking lot. "Should have picked up my prescription yesterday. A little sinus problem," he explained. "I was supposed to take the first pill this morning. Is it still morning?" He started to climb out of the car.

"Sorry!" Hannah replied, looking at her watch. "You've missed it by two hours, eleven minutes, and thirty-two seconds."

"So precise!" He smiled. "I'll leave the car running so you'll have air conditioning."

"Thanks!" She glanced at the time-temperature sign in front of the bank across the street. "It's eighty-four degrees outside."

"This shouldn't take long."

She watched him enter the store, and then had a sudden, irreverent thought. *An opportunity! Can I do it in time?* Quickly, she turned on the radio, then pushed the release button on the glove box. *Locked.* After another glance at the entrance, she slipped a small, slim tool out of her purse where it had been resting alongside her knife. In seconds the glove box was open, the lock undamaged, and the tool was back in her purse.

Inside she found only a blank notepad and pen, and a small leather folder. Keeping an eye on the store's entrance, she opened the folder. Just two items: an insurance card for the Mercedes she was sitting in, and a Georgia driver's license. The photo on the license was Martin's, but the name on it was ... Richard Morrison? Just then Martin exited the store. *Oh no!* Hannah quickly memorized "Richard Morrison's" date of birth, replaced everything exactly as it had been, shut the box, and started swaying in time with the music on the radio.

"Told you it wouldn't take long," Martin said, sliding into the driver's seat, "but I see you weren't bored anyway."

"Not a bit. I turned on the radio, and Johnny Cash was right there singing to me. I don't recognize the guy who's singing now."

"That, my dear, is a very popular up-and-comer named Keith Urban."

"Nice. I gather you like country music."

"Mmhm. That's my favorite radio station."

At the restaurant, they ordered tacos and senior drinks, and Hannah scanned the room for Suzy Carlson's teenagers to see if they were giggling with their friends in a corner booth. One of their friends, the blond girl, would be easy to spot. She had one of those spiky haircuts that made her look like she'd stuck her thumb in an electric socket. *No, they're not here today. Good!*

"Tell me what you've been up to, Hannah," Martin said after he'd taken his first bite. "Your daily phone calls only gave me the basics, left a lot for me to worry about. Did you girls do anything dangerous? Like, maybe, sky-diving?"

Hannah laughed. "Nothing dangerous, unless you call *shopping* dangerous."

"Now *that's* an extreme sport! Count me out!"

Hannah was quick on the uptake: "Aren't you the one who said, 'You'd be surprised what you'll do if given a challenge'? There you go!"

He made a face. "Anything but shopping."

"Don't worry; I won't challenge you. Now let me tell you about having lots of fun—the 'girl' kind!"

And she gave him a detailed account of her *fabulous* shopping trip; her *wonderful* overnight visit with friends in Fort Valley; their evening of *partying*; and a *fantastic* day at an outdoor barbecue. All very *special*, she told him, because it had been a long time since she'd seen those particular friends. In other words, she fed him a load of shit. *Back at you, Martin!*

After they finished lunch, he suggested ice cream cones from the Baskin-Robbins shop next to the park.

"You sure know the way to a girl's heart," she said.

"I hope so," he replied. "At least to *this* girl's heart," he added softly.

His words, his voice, sounded so sincere that Hannah had difficulty accepting that this was just business to him. Or was it? If not, was his job more important than his feelings for her? She considered her own situation and admitted that, yes, the job was more important. For her, it always had been that way with no regrets. She would be forever grateful to the U.S.A. for taking the lead in ending the killing of so many innocent people—*her* people. She had eagerly given the best years of her life to the CIA. Now, she would take the chip off her shoulder and forget about her comfortable, cozy, retirement life—certainly a life without Martin—to stop a threat to the future of her adopted country. Any threat, no matter how small, was worth dying for, if that's what it would take.

They took their cones into the park and found a bench under a shade tree. Hannah started the conversation with a comment about how busy the food bank volunteers were that morning. Then she said, "You know, the women workers don't like your friend Paul Smith very much."

He looked at her, raising his eyebrows. "Friend? Paul's not my friend, just a co-worker. Or, I should say a 'co-volunteer.'"

"But you guys always pair off that way—Bob and Brad, you and Paul."

"That's the way guys are." He shrugged. "Creatures of habit."

She faked a laugh. "Yeah, well, Paul's got some very bad habits."

"Ugh. Don't remind me! A couple of weeks ago he said something that offended Bob, and Bob told him off. That surprised me, 'cause Bob's usually so mild-mannered."

"Now that you mention it, Bob and Brad have moved a little farther down the room, away from the two of you. I'd hoped it wasn't because of you!"

He grinned. "Yeah, me too! Actually, I don't know much about Paul. He said he moved here ten years ago to help save a friend's failing auto shop. When the business improved, he decided to retire in Meadow Bridge. Anyway, the men who volunteer are pretty quiet, different from those women you hang out with. Y'all are a noisy bunch!"

This time Hannah's laughter was real. "Hey, careful there, or you'll end up with ice cream in your face!"

Conversation remained light and friendly, as they both played their parts, avoiding personal things, issues they both knew they faced. She had discovered his secret, and was fairly certain he had discovered hers—that she was a retired agent. Or at least he was well into the process of discovering it. What did he intend to do with that information? Anything? Nothing? And to complicate the situation even further, there was no doubt that deep feelings for each other ignited whenever they were together. Like now. Despite her strong will to remain focused and maintain distance, Hannah felt her heart racing in his presence and knew Martin felt the same. This was not an act. She also knew that a deep chasm was opening between them, and there was not one thing she could, or would, do to stop it.

Chapter 20

Martin drove Hannah back to the food bank parking lot where she'd left her car. He seemed reluctant to say goodbye, but Hannah didn't linger. She gave him a quick, friendly hug and was off and away.

A few minutes later she pulled into her driveway. As she stepped out of her car, she spotted Rachel Krenshaw fast-walking toward her. But this time, rather than retreating, she decided to do a little sleuthing. She waved, and Rachel slowed down, coming to a stop at the end of Hannah's walkway. She was breathing heavily.

"Hello, Hannah!" She breathed in and out noisily. "I've already been down and back three times, and I'm finally tired!"

"Would you like a cold drink?"

"Perfect!" More hard breathing.

"Come and sit. I'll get us some water." Hannah went inside and returned quickly with a pitcher of water and two glasses. Her guest was already seated, her breathing nearly under control.

"It's not quite as hot today as it's been," Rachel offered. "I guess that rain we had earlier cooled things off." She drank thirstily from her glass. "And I thank you for cooling *me* off!"

"My pleasure," Hannah answered, echoing the phrase she'd learned to appreciate. "Rachel," she said, as she took a chair across the table, "when you catch your breath, please tell me a little more about your Polo meetings. I know I said

I wasn't interested, but I've been thinking about it, and maybe politics is something I should take more of an interest in. After all, getting involved is the right way to make changes for the good of everyone." *Hope I don't sound too naïve,* she thought.

"Oh, Hannah, you'd like Polo; I know you would. In fact, I had planned to invite you again and again, until you got so annoyed with me that you'd give in and come to a meeting!" She laughed at her own humor, and Hannah smiled in return, already annoyed. "Seriously, you're always doing good things like volunteering at the food bank and helping other people," Rachel continued. "I saw you the other day at Walmart helping that lady who couldn't remember where she'd parked her car. You talked with her and figured it out and took her right to it. And I'm sure you didn't even know her!"

Hannah put on a shy face. "I didn't realize anyone saw me. I just did what my conscience told me to do."

"That's just it. You *care.* And that's what Polo is all about—caring about our world and trying to make a difference."

"So … what do you discuss?"

"Anything political, but mostly about government—what's right with it, and what's wrong with it. Believe me, there's a *lot* wrong. We study other countries' governments too, and make comparisons. Honestly, you'd be good for us, Hannah. You're smart, and you don't hesitate to speak your mind."

Hannah laughed. "Sometimes that works against me. But, yes, I'd like to give it a try. When is your next meeting?"

"Not until next month, I'm sorry to say. We just met last week. Had a good conversation going, good ideas." She gave Hannah the date, time and place, and Hannah memorized it. "May I pick you up?"

"That's a nice offer, Rachel, but I'd rather drive myself, if that's okay."

"See? You spoke your mind just then! And I admire that." When she finally finished talking and rose to leave, she repeated the meeting information and said goodbye. "I'll see you next month if not sooner!"

Hannah waved, making a mental note: *Tell Doc about Rachel and the Polos.*

Later that evening she drove to the supermarket to pick up a few groceries. Most important, she was out of Diet Pepsi, which she considered a "staple." She had put a few items in her cart and was moving slowly toward the produce section, when she spotted Art Lansfeldt picking through the bananas. He was inspecting each one, like a fussy old crone. *Serendipity*, she thought. *This is my chance.*

"Well hello, Art. Imagine meeting you here!"

His head swiveled on his neck and he gave her a blank stare.

She smiled brightly and reached out. "I'm Hannah. From the book club!"

He looked at her hand, then shook it briefly, without enthusiasm.

"How do the bananas look to you?" she asked. "I need a few, too."

"They're okay." He turned his attention back to the bananas.

Hannah's attention remained on him—his lack of personality, his skinny body and bloodless complexion. *Yes, he's weird*, she thought. But she persisted. "You seem to know what you're doing, Art. Would you mind picking out three good bananas for me? I always manage to choose the wrong ones, and when I start to peel one, it's either too ripe or too green."

He selected three and, with a sharp nod, handed them to her.

"Oh, thank you so much! By the way, I enjoyed the discussion of Frank McCourt's *'Tis* at our last meeting, and I noticed you had some very thoughtful comments about it. You must have liked the book."

To her surprise, Art turned to face her, and his eyes brightened, though he still spoke in that expressionless voice. "Yes, I did," he said. "I enjoy positive stories, like that one, rather than negative, depressing ones like that horrible 'true crime' novel last month. We have enough misery in this world without inviting it into our lives." He turned back to the fruit, effectively ending the conversation, in which he'd spoken more words than Hannah had ever heard him say at one time!

"Well, it was nice seeing you, Art. See you at the next meeting!"

He nodded without looking at her, and she moved on toward the check-out.

Eloise had called him "creepy," an apt assessment. But his comments about negativity and misery, and his preference for uplifting stories, started Hannah thinking.

Maybe there's more to Art Lansfeldt than the impression he leaves with people. Something much deeper? ... If Art is a sleeper agent, he's certainly an unusual one. No enthusiasm for his job or anything else. If he's tasked with gathering info or recruiting, he's bound to fail. ... Maybe that's what he wants. Maybe he's involved in something he'd rather not be doing and is hoping to be reassigned or retired. Is Martin trying to keep him in the game? Or help him exit? ... Or worse?

Chapter 21

Next morning when Hannah arrived at the gym, Martin was walking on a treadmill. He waved her over. "I won't be in class this morning," he said, still walking and breathing hard. "Leaving here in a few minutes. Quick shower. Spending the rest of the day in Perry. Kiwanis meeting at lunch. Afternoon and evening with friends."

"We'll miss you," she said. She gave him a quick wave and headed for class.

After stretching and warm-ups, the music's tempo picked up and aerobics began. As the early rock sounds of Buddy Holley blasted over the speakers, Hannah's brain kicked into high gear, moving as fast as her legs, feet and arms. She made more mental notes: *Check Kiwanis meeting time and membership. Who does Martin hang out with in the gym when he's not in class? Have Doc check out Art Lansfeldt and Paul Smith. Why does Anne Hargesty always end up on Martin's other side when he's sitting with me in church? Does he see her at other times? Check.*

He called her late that afternoon to say his friends—old buddies from college—wanted him to stay for the whole weekend. They'd made plans to attend an autocross event and other things that Hannah paid very little attention to, because she assumed they were lies. Like the big one: *He was calling from Perry, but he sure didn't go to a Kiwanis meeting there!* Perry's Kiwanians met for lunch on Tuesdays. She'd checked. Today was Friday.

If Martin was a good, sharp foreign agent—and now she had no doubt he was, especially after seeing that fake driver's license—why did he make such a stupid error with the Kiwanis meeting? ... He didn't. It had to be intentional. *He wanted me to catch it. Will he make an excuse, saying it wasn't Kiwanis but something else and he'd confused the two? Or does he hope we'll confess to each other, bare our souls, and "ride off into the sunset" together, forever in hiding?*

She hated herself for thinking that was an option. But it could have been, once upon a time. Dare she admit to herself that she might have loved him? Did she still? How could she love someone and hate what he was? Was that possible? She was certain he loved her; women *know* those things. That's one area where men cannot deceive. And she was equally certain that he, like she, had a job to do. Which would be more important to him? If it came to a choice, she already knew which would be more important to her. Nothing could change her mind. Not even love.

~~~~~

Sunday was a beautiful day, a good day for getting dressed up and going to church, which Hannah did. The choir entered during the prelude and took their seats in the chancel. Hannah spotted Rachel Krenshaw and, again, was glad she wouldn't be sitting up there beside her. Since Martin wouldn't be in church today—still off for the weekend—she was hoping to see Anne Hargesty and do a little reconnaissance. She looked around. Still no Anne. Finally, the woman slid into the pew beside her just as the prelude ended. Anne whispered, "Where's Martin?"

"Visiting friends for the weekend," she whispered back.

The service started then, and Anne offered to share her hymnal with Hannah. Hannah's singing voice was good, but she was dismayed (envious?) to hear Anne's clear, accurate alto beside her, the same lovely harmonies Martin must have heard on several Sundays.

Together, they walked to the parking lot following the service, and Hannah asked, "Would you like to have lunch with me, Anne? Or do you have other plans?"

"Oh, that sounds wonderful!" she replied. "Sundays can be very lonely."

They didn't know each other well, just meeting once a week in church, exchanging pleasantries—a comment or two on the sermon or the weather.

Hannah suggested a Mexican restaurant in nearby Fort Valley, where they found a comfortable booth and an accommodating server.

After they'd ordered, Hannah asked, "How long have you lived in Meadow Bridge, Anne? I don't recall seeing you in church before the past year or so."

"I've been here ten months, but I just started attending church regularly three months ago. What about you, Hannah? Have you been in Meadow Bridge long? It's such a nice little town!"

"It is nice," Hannah replied. "I've lived there almost thirty years. My late husband is buried in Meadow Bridge, and I have no desire to leave."

"Your late husband? I'm sorry, Hannah."

"Don't be," Hannah assured her. "We had a wonderful life together."

Anne still looked apologetic. "Well, I kind of thought that you and Martin were a couple. You're always together in church."

"Just good friends." Their food arrived then, and they began eating. "Tell me about yourself, Anne," Hannah said. "Do you work somewhere?"

"Retired. I volunteer at the animal shelter."

"That's nice. What made you choose Meadow Bridge for your retirement?"

Anne looked down at her plate, blinked her eyes, and sighed.

"Hey, Anne, you don't have to tell me," Hannah said. "It's okay."

"No, I want to." She looked up at Hannah. "You and Martin have always been kind and friendly after church. I guess that's why I keep returning to the same pew to sit by you. And now you've invited me to lunch. You see, I don't … I don't talk much with people. Just animals," she added with a shy smile. "You asked how I chose Meadow Bridge. I didn't really choose it. I'd been out driving one day for several hours, in no particular direction, and ended up in Meadow Bridge. It attracted me right away, so quaint, plus the fact that it's many miles away from Dillard up in the mountains. That's a *good* thing." She paused and sipped her iced tea. And Hannah waited. Anne spoke slowly. "I was running, Hannah. Running from an abusive husband. He was particularly abusive emotionally; he liked to make me feel stupid and unworthy of him. But he also got physical once in a while—a few bruises, a broken arm."

Just the thought of such abuse from a husband was appalling to Hannah, who'd only known tenderness and love from David.

Anne's eyes filled with tears, and Hannah handed her a tissue. "I just couldn't take it any longer. And I thank God that we didn't have children." She sighed. "I should feel terrible saying this, Hannah, but I was glad when I heard that his car slammed into a tree and he was killed. That happened just a few weeks after I'd left him. He'd often had road rage. Maybe that last time he was raging at me and took his anger out on the car. Or the tree."

Hannah reached over and put her hand over Anne's hand. "Better that way than on you," she said.

Anne smiled gratefully, as if Hannah were a long lost friend. "Thank you," she said. "I didn't want to go back to Dillard to live. There's nothing there for me, no family, very few friends, just bad memories. I only went back once, to choose a few things to move—the rest went to charity—and I put the house on the market. It finally sold last month."

"Well, you're at home now," Hannah said, encouragingly. "Anne, have you considered joining the church choir? When you and I were sharing a hymnal this morning, I noticed your lovely alto voice. The director would be very happy to have you as a member, believe me!"

"You really think so?"

"I know so. I could tell him about your voice and how lucky he'd be to get you!" Hannah smiled and winked. "I substitute in the choir sometimes, and I'd be happy to take you to your first rehearsal."

Anne's eyes grew wide. "You would? You would do that for me?" Hannah nodded. "Oh, Hannah, I've wanted to be in that choir ever since I started attending church, but I thought ..." She looked down. "I thought they probably wouldn't want me. I was afraid to ask."

"Well, I'll arrange it for you, and I'll pick you up Wednesday at seven o'clock for rehearsal. Okay?"

Hannah thought if Anne could have jumped over the table and hugged her, she probably would have done it. "Yes!" Anne replied. "Thank you!"

At least Anne won't have to sit near Rachel, since Anne is an alto and Rachel sings soprano.

They exchanged phone numbers, and stayed a while longer, talking about pleasant things. Anne obviously loved her work at the shelter. And Hannah related some of her own story (cover story, of course). Anne seemed relieved to have found a friend.

Hannah, well, Hannah didn't know what to think.

Chapter 22

When she arrived home, she changed into comfortable clothes and called Doc. It was time to give him some names, let his team dig for the truth.

"This is Sunday, Hannah," he said.

"I'm working, and so can you." She heard a snort on the other end.

"I have some names."

"How sure are you?"

"Ninety-nine percent on some; fifty on the others."

"Go ahead."

"In no particular order: Paul Smith. Common name, but the food bank database has him on Early Avenue, Meadow Bridge; Art Lansfeldt, L-a-n-s-f-e-l-d-t, the only one in town with that surname; and Anne Hargesty, H-a-r-g-e-s-t-y, originally from Dillard, Georgia. Also Martin's golf buddies. They're together on the golf course every Saturday morning without fail." She gave him their names.

"Nice, inconspicuous way to meet and talk."

"There are two more. See what you can find on Richard Morrison, date of birth—four, fourteen, nineteen forty-two." (She was glad that one had been easy to memorize—four, four, four!)

"Who is he?"

"I'm not sure. I saw his name on some paperwork that caught my attention."

"Not going to tell me what paperwork?"

"Not yet. The other name is Rachel Krenshaw, with a K. She lives on my street, a few blocks east. She belongs to what she calls a 'political discussion group,' which sounded suspicious when she described it to me. They call it Polo. And she's trying to recruit me. Their next meeting is about four weeks away, and I told her I'd be there."

"Don't worry, Hannah. If we discover they're a cell, they won't be there in four weeks."

"What about me?" she asked reluctantly. "Will I be here in four weeks?"

"You know the rules, Hannah."

Yes, I know the rules.

~~~~~~

Shortly after her conversation with Doc ended, she stepped out onto the front porch and Suzy Carlson came running across the street clutching a newspaper. "Have you seen today's paper, Hannah?" she called out.

"Haven't had time. I've been to Sunday School and church, and then I had lunch with a new friend. Did something interesting happen?"

"Something sad, if you ask me. It's all right here," she said, poking at her paper. "I'm afraid it's about someone you know."

"What? Who?"

"Let's sit on your porch for a few minutes. Come on." Suzy led the way to the little table and chairs, and they sat.

Now Hannah was really concerned. "What happened, Suzy?"

"I don't know the man, but Betty called me as soon as she saw the article. She said he's in the book club with you. His name is Art Lansfeldt, and he died in a terrible accident."

"Oh, no!" Hannah felt more than sadness; she felt fear. She leaned back in her chair. "Tell me about it, please."

"Well, it happened last night. He was riding his motorcycle on a paved road out in the country—It seems that was his hobby, motorcycle riding—and as he went over a rise in the road, he hit something hard that was directly in his path. Turns out it was some cement blocks, those things they use to build foundations with? Anyway, the collision sent him flying over the top of his motorcycle and head first onto the concrete. He wasn't wearing a helmet." She reached across the small table and patted Hannah's hand. "I'm sorry, dear. I know that all of you book clubbers are friends."

"It's all right. ... I'm all right. It's just such a shock, you know."

Suzy nodded. "The article says he rode the same route every night, so the blocks must have fallen into the road during the day, probably from one of those dreadfully overloaded pickup trucks headed for the landfill. ... So sad."

"I'm glad you told me, Suzy. That was much better than reading about it in the paper. Were there any other details?"

"Only that they're trying to locate his family."

Hannah thanked Suzy again and excused herself. It had been a long day.

As she changed into more comfortable clothes, she deliberately calmed her mind and her senses. To think rationally. First of all, riding a motorcycle was the *last* thing she would have expected of Art Lansfeldt. He didn't fit the stereotype. But then, nothing about him had rung true. *Think, Hannah! He rode the same route every night—his routine was predictable. Cement blocks "fell" from a pickup truck onto the exact spot where he would hit them? Not likely. And no other vehicles hit them first. Did someone place those blocks there at precisely the right time? Or was the accident staged? Were the blocks placed there* after *Art had been killed? I'm glad Martin is away for the weekend*, she thought. *That means he didn't do it. Wonder if he knows about it yet?* She considered another possibility: *Did Martin plan the job and assign it to someone else? ... Now there's an evil thought.*

Hannah, determined to relax, changed into comfortable clothes and put one of her favorite CDs on the stereo— Danny Wright's "Black and White" piano music—and stretched out on the living room sofa with Sunday's *Atlanta Journal-Constitution*. The first sentence she read was not conducive to relaxation. "The federal government is eyeing the Savannah River Site for a new multibillion-dollar plant that would build atomic bombs." The site was in South Carolina near Augusta, Georgia; and Augusta was a mere 150 miles from Meadow Bridge. Hannah understood that these particular bombs, used in thermonuclear warheads, were necessary for the safety and security of the United States. She just didn't like thinking about it, especially having them so close to home. Over the years she'd come to regard her adopted town as insulated. Not *isolated*, but insulated from the worries of the world. The article went on to say that, according to an Energy Department statement, production would begin in 2020. *That's eighteen years from now,* she thought. *I'll surely be dead by then and it won't matter to me!* Gloomy news. However, she remembered being delighted with something she'd read a few days earlier. For the first time in Georgia, a woman—Brigadier General Janet Hicks—was named by the Pentagon to command a major military installation. *Yea! Way to go!* Hannah Rosse admired strong women.

~~~~~

Martin wasn't at the gym on Monday when Hannah arrived, but he did show up in time for class. After the workout, he walked with her toward the locker rooms. "Donnalee's tonight?" he asked. The sweet smile she had started to love was on his face.

"I'm warning you, I'll be hungry," she answered.

"Me, too. I'll pick you up at six-thirty." He had not said a word about Art's death. *Maybe he doesn't know yet.* She was hopeful.

Hannah dressed for the evening in a pretty pantsuit with nice jewelry. She still cared for Martin and wanted to impress him, even though she knew he was the enemy.

He rang her doorbell at exactly six-thirty; and, as they approached his car, he said, "I picked up some strays along the way. Hope you don't mind."

She looked into the backseat and saw Jeff and Shelly Karroll smiling and waving to her. "What a nice surprise!" she said as she slid into the passenger seat. "Martin didn't tell me you were coming, but I'm glad you're here!"

Jeff grinned. "Yeah, ol' Martin dragged us along at the last minute."

"We were talking with him on the phone," Shelly explained, "and he mentioned going to your favorite restaurant tonight. Then he must have felt obligated to invite us."

"An' we felt *obligated* to accept," Jeff added.

By then, they were all laughing, and Martin started the car.

Donnalee's was fairly busy for a Monday night, but they found a table in a quiet corner and ordered the latest chicken creation. This time it had a delicious honey glaze—not honey barbecue—just honey, flavored with an undetermined array of spices that left Hannah wishing for more.

Jeff said it was *heaven*. "Why in the world is this place called Donnalee's?" he asked as he ate. "It ought to be 'Chicken Heaven,' or 'Heavenly Chicken.'"

"Jeff," Shelly said, sighing, "don't you suppose the owner is named Donnalee? That would be logical, wouldn't it?"

"Who cares 'bout logic?"

"Actually, Shelly, you're wrong," Hannah said. "Miriam Johnson owns the restaurant, and Donnalee is the name of Meadow Bridge's one claim to fame—she's our only, ever, champion mud wrestler! She won her trophy back in the sixties."

"Right on!" Jeff cheered, a little too loudly.

Martin laughed. "I never heard that story!"

"It's true. She was Miriam's grandmother."

Then Shelly asked, innocently, "What is a mud wrestler?" Giggles erupted as they explained the sport to her.

They continued eating, and Martin ordered an extra plate of chicken for Jeff and him to share.

"Hannah, tell us about yourself," Shelly said. "Have you lived in Meadow Bridge all your life?"

"Oh, no. Although sometimes it seems like it. I feel very much at home here." She wiped her mouth with a napkin. "As a child, I lived in Alabama with my parents, but we moved around the state quite often. Never stayed more than two years in one place. My father was an itinerant handyman, and we followed builders and contractors to wherever the jobs were. Then we went to Texas under the same circumstances. So you can see why I like living in Meadow Bridge. Thirty years in one place!"

"I do understand." Shelly turned her attention to her husband and whispered, "Jeff, try not to make so much noise when you eat!"

"Cain't help it. I'm in heaven!"

Martin laughed. "Leave the boy alone, Shel."

"Well, just *try*, Jeff," Shelly pleaded. "Okay?"

"I might could," he replied, grinning.

Hannah smiled to herself. That was one southern expression she'd never made sense of, even after hearing it once or twice a week for thirty years. Might could. Did that mean he *might* try, or he *could* try? Yes, she loved Meadow Bridge, the southern people, and their friendly, folksy ways. She hoped she'd never have to leave it!

After Martin and Jeff finished their shared plate, Hannah asked, "Jeff, I have no doubt you've lived in Georgia all your life. You *sound* like you belong, and I mean that as a compliment. Have you always been in the same area?"

He smiled and answered proudly, "Same area, same farm, and same house!"

"Really?" Hannah was surprised. "I can't imagine such a steady life."

"That house me and Shelly live in? I was *born* there. Belonged to my grandpa, my daddy, an' now me. O' course it's gone through some renovations over the years."

"And it's beautiful," Hannah said. "I can't believe it will soon be one-hundred years old."

"We love it," Shelly said. "When Jeff and I were dating, he told me he never wanted to live anywhere else, and that was just fine with me!"

"So when I asked her to marry me, she already knew it was either me *and* the house, or …"

"Or nothing." Shelly laughed and slapped Jeff on the shoulder. "How could I say no to such an offer?"

Martin thought that was funny and said, "At least he didn't offer you himself *or* the house."

"Yeah," Jeff said. "She'd probably have taken my house!"

Hannah was enjoying their easy banter. "How long have you two been married?" she asked.

"A lonnnng time," Jeff answered, dragging it out.

"Just eight years," Shelly said. "Eight *long* years!"

And so their fun-filled conversation continued. Hannah enjoyed every minute of the evening, and when they drove her home she said, sincerely, "I had a wonderful time! I'm really glad Martin 'dragged' you two along, and I hope he does it again real soon!"

"Count on it," Martin said as he climbed out of the car. He walked her to the door; and, yes, he kissed her, though it was quick. And they heard Jeff's loud whistle from the car!

She had not mentioned Art's death. With Jeff and Shelly present the entire evening, it would not have been a smart thing to do.

~~~~~

Hannah needed the answers to a couple of big questions, but there was no one she could ask. She had to ferret them on her own. She was fairly certain the Karrolls were sleepers, but she also liked being with them. They were fun. And again she reminded herself, *that's what sleepers do. They blend into the company of others and are often well liked.* That didn't hold true, though, for Paul Smith and Art Lansfeldt. Paul tried, but his method wasn't working. Art hadn't even tried.

Her questions: *Are Jeff and Shelly both sleepers, or just Shelly? If just Shelly, does Jeff know about it? Did she recruit Jeff?*

Hannah was surprised that Jeff still lived on the property where he was born. That could not possibly be a lie, because it would be too easy to check. *Easy to check?* Those words triggered a thought that had somehow escaped her: *Why had Martin made up that story about Monkey's Eyebrow, Kentucky? Surely he knew that would be easy to check! If he did it intentionally, why? To what purpose? Did he* want *to be caught?* Hannah's "logic" was spinning out of control.

Chapter 23

Hannah didn't hear from Martin the next day, but on Wednesday morning the aerobics class was in full swing when she arrived several minutes late. She quickly claimed a spot and joined in the twisting moves of their exaggerated and energetic cha-cha. The mirrored wall at the front of the class showed about twenty women and five or six men working hard and having a great time. The instructor was front and center, facing the mirror where she could watch everyone as she led the movements. The members' age range was wide, from late forties to early seventies, plus one active eighty-year-old. And not a slacker in the bunch!

Martin was there, and he gave Hannah a big smile through the mirror. She returned it. Class finished at noon, and they walked together toward the locker rooms.

"Did you oversleep?" he asked.

"Me? Oversleep? No way! I left on time but got caught in a traffic jam. Somehow, a truck ended up crosswise on Murdock Street. There were a lot of cars behind it, including mine, and nobody could move until it was pulled out of the way." She paused, then added, "I was tired before I got here; now I'm exhausted!"

"Poor thing!" he said with mock sympathy. "Would a sandwich perk you up?" He named the place.

She laughed. "Let's find out. Give me thirty minutes to get cleaned up and I'll meet you there."

After showering and changing, Hannah left the gym to find a light rain falling—not a storm, just a pleasant sprinkle.

She was glad to see Martin already seated at the restaurant with their favorite drinks in front of him.

"I didn't order yet, because I didn't know what you'd want," he said. So she told him, and he went to get their food.

"Seems like we do a lot of eating out lately," Hannah said when he returned. She was smiling. "But I'm not complaining!"

"Hope not, 'cause I really enjoy our meals together. Even these little ones," he added, placing a tray in front of her.

Hannah was happy, yet she wasn't. Each day she was more and more torn between Good Martin and Bad Martin. She loved the good and despised the bad. The end was near, and it didn't look promising.

"You must tell me all about your wild weekend," she said as they ate, anticipating his lies.

"Yeah. Well, I got mixed up on the Kiwanis meeting day. Must have been thinking too much about you," he said with a wink.

So much for riding off into the sunset.

"So I had a burger and fries," he continued. "I know, I know. That's not healthy. But it sure tasted good! And then I went to the library until time to meet my friends."

"What did you do at the library?"

"Read magazines, mostly. And I flipped through a copy of Norman Vincent Peale's *The Power of Positive Thinking.* Good book. How did you pass the weekend, Hannah?"

"Household chores on Saturday. Sunday I went to church and then had lunch with Anne." She took another bite of her tuna salad sandwich.

He looked up. "Anne Hargesty?"

Hannah nodded.

"I'd have thought she'd be too boring for you," he said.

"Is that supposed to be a compliment?"

He grinned. "Sure."

"Actually, she was very good company. Anne is a lonely person. She needs a friend."

Martin shrugged indifferently. "She's so quiet. What in the world did you two find to talk about?"

"Not about *you*, if that's what you're thinking," she teased, and he made a face. She wondered if he were checking up on Anne. Or on her. "We talked about her work at the animal shelter. Anne's not at all shy when discussing animals." Hannah ate the last bite of her sandwich and wiped her mouth. "I want to hear about the autocross and the other exciting things you and your friends did."

He described the autocross event in great detail, which was probably true, and then told her about the other places they went, which were probably not true.

"But you had to miss playing golf Saturday morning. That's unusual for you. What did your golf buddies do without you?"

"Oh, there's no shortage of players. Someone's always in the clubhouse hoping to join a foursome."

"Martin," Hannah said quietly, as they sipped their drinks. "Did you know … Have you heard about Art?"

He sighed and nodded his head. "It's so sad—killed in an accident Saturday night. You heard how it happened?"

"Yes. His motorcycle hit cement blocks on a country road at night." She rolled her eyes. "Really, that is *unbelievable*." She watched for Martin's reaction—there was none—and then added, "The authorities have been trying to locate his family."

"Art was an okay guy, a little strange. But I wouldn't wish that kind of death on anyone."

"Did you know he rode a motorcycle?"

He nodded. "We'd talked about it. He probably talked with me more than with anyone else, and that wasn't much. You said they're trying to find his family. The only family he has—had—is a brother in Indiana. Guess I'd better see what I can do to help."

"That would be nice. I'm sorry Martin. I know he considered you his friend."

Hannah had been looking for a tell-tale reaction from Martin, but none was forthcoming. He had simply acted as one would have expected Martin Wynn to ... *act*.

As they left the restaurant, Martin said quietly to Hannah, "I have ice cream at home in the fridge."

She smiled, glad he had lightened the mood. "So do I."

They went to Hannah's house and sat in the kitchen with their ice cream—chocolate, of course. The conversation was light, no probing questions from either side. When they finished, he stood, came behind her chair, and began massaging her neck and shoulders.

"Ooo, what made you decide I need this wonderful treatment?"

"The other day, when I told you about June's massage appointment, you said, 'Mmm. Sounds nice.' So I thought you might like this little half-massage."

"I do, I do!"

After a few minutes, he stopped. "Time for me to go," he said, abruptly. "It's been a very nice day." He pulled her to her feet and they walked to the door.

Martin spoke first, slowly and softly. "I ... I think I'm falling in love with you, Hannah."

She leaned her head onto his chest but couldn't bring herself to say the words.

He lifted her chin, kissed her lips and her forehead. And left.

~~~~~~

That evening at 7:00 Hannah picked Anne up for choir rehearsal, glad for the distraction, because Martin's words had been going over and over in her head.

On the previous day she had talked with the music director, Scott Ansley, and he was eager to meet Anne. Scott was young—in his early forties, which was young to Hannah—and not only was he an excellent musician, he also was good with people.

Anne was obviously nervous. She kept patting her hair as they drove to the church.

Hannah tried to reassure her. "I know you'll enjoy the other choir members once you get to know them, Anne. They're all very welcoming and friendly. Scott, in particular, is looking forward to having you in the alto section."

"Really?"

"Really. I told him how well you sing, but even if you didn't, it would not matter because there are no auditions. Everyone who wants to be part of the group is welcome."

Anne seemed to relax a little. "Will you be staying, Hannah?" she asked.

"Of course!" Hannah laughed. "Did you think I'd just dump you there?"

Anne smiled. "No. You're really sweet to do this. I appreciate it very much."

"I'll be watching and listening and enjoying the music!"

As it turned out, Scott asked Hannah if she could possibly substitute this Sunday in the soprano section. Rachel Krenshaw had a conflict and couldn't be there.

Hannah joined the evening rehearsal and had a wonderful time. Especially since Rachel was absent!

Chapter 24

The next day, as Hanna entered the food bank workers' area, Barbara came running up to her. "Hannah, there's an antique show at the Georgia State Fairgrounds in Perry this week, and I really want to attend! I've already asked Eloise and June, and they'd like to go tomorrow and stay through Saturday. Will you join us? Let's make a party of it!"

"Yeah! C'mon, Hannah. Let's do it!" Eloise cried.

"We'll have fun," June said, encouragingly.

Hannah laughed. "You know I never turn down an invitation."

"Great! I'll pick you up at noon tomorrow. We'll spend the night in a cheap motel—I've already made reservations. And we'll come home Saturday night."

Hannah was glad to go with the girls for more than one reason. She knew they'd have a great time; and, the trip would give her two days to recover from Martin's declaration of love. This time, she wouldn't have to lie to him about where she'd been and what she'd done. It would be fun to go and fun to talk about it afterward!

Eloise rode in front with Barbara, and June and Hannah were in the backseat. Hannah had always enjoyed looking at antiques, especially furniture, but she didn't own any and never would. She needed to keep her home furnished simply and inexpensively to blend in with the neighborhood and not draw attention to herself. June loved looking at, but not buying, 1950s retro items reminiscent of her teenage years; and Barbara and Eloise loved bargains, no matter what kind!

Each of them had a good sense of humor, particularly when they were together, and Hannah was excited about the getaway.

The "cheap motel" Barbara had reserved for them was … well, cheap. The light bulbs were dim, the bars of soap were no bigger than a half-dollar, and the idea of an in-room coffee pot was pure fantasy. But none of that mattered. The room was clean; and, after walking through the huge showrooms for five hours and gorging at a local barbecue restaurant, the room was a welcome retreat. The "girls" giggled themselves to sleep.

The next day they went back to the show. June asked, rather cautiously, "Are you sure there're more rooms? Didn't we see it all yesterday?"

"Yes, we saw it all," Barbara answered, "but yesterday we were just looking."

"Today we're shopping!" Eloise said with glee.

Hannah laughed. "Will June and I have to share the backseat with a huge coffee table or maybe a lamp with a wobbly shade?"

"Probably. You girls are both small, so it shouldn't be a problem."

"Oh boy," was June's comment.

They did have a great time, and all of the "stuff" Eloise and Barbara bought fit nicely into the trunk. Except a china turkey platter, which rested between Hannah and June, well protected!

Hannah looked forward to telling Martin about all the fun they'd had. … But he never asked her about those two days.

~~~~~

On Sunday morning Hannah and Anne entered with the choir during the prelude, Anne in the alto section and Hannah with the sopranos. Hannah looked out toward her familiar place in the congregation and spotted Martin, alone and bewildered. She had not told him she'd be singing, and he had not yet noticed her in the choir. When he did, his mouth dropped open in surprise, and he quickly covered it with one hand. Then his hand came down to reveal a bright smile. She returned his smile. The congregation rose to sing the opening hymn, and from behind his hymnal, Martin gave her a discreet "thumbs up." The choir selection was "God So Loved the World," a beautiful a cappella anthem by John Stainer. They sang it well.

After the service, Martin was waiting in the parking lot when Hannah and Anne emerged. "You didn't tell me you'd be singing today," he said. "What a nice surprise!"

"I didn't know until Wednesday evening when I took Anne to rehearsal and got recruited. It was just for this week, as a substitute. But Anne is now a regular member of the choir!"

"Congratulations, Anne," Martin said. "Both of you ladies looked great up there in your robes and stoles."

Anne smiled shyly and said, "Thank you, Martin." She turned to Hannah. "And thank *you*, Hannah, for encouraging me and getting me involved. I haven't been this happy in a long time!"

They chatted for a few minutes, then Anne excused herself and hurried off to her car. Hannah's "other self" had been watching carefully for any undercurrent that might have flowed between Anne and Martin; but if it existed, she could not detect it.

They parted ways, Hannah saying she was expected at Suzy's for lunch, which was true. Martin looked disappointed, but he put on a brave face and walked to his car, waving and smiling.

~~~~~

Martin didn't appear at the gym on Monday, and Hannah played hooky on Wednesday, so the next time they saw each other was Thursday morning at the food bank. Hannah arrived on time, but Martin was not there yet. June and Eloise were just getting things organized, and June was talking about their trip to the antique show on the previous Friday and Saturday.

"I was absolutely exhausted when we got home Saturday night!" she exclaimed.

"So was I," Eloise said. "And I still am," she added with a wry grin. "But I'll pretend I'm not. What about you, Hannah?"

"Actually, I feel energized."

"Hey, I heard that!" Paul Smith called out, walking toward the women. "I feel energized too! What d'ya say we go out back and work off some of that energy?" He wiggled his butt. "Any takers?"

The other three women turned away, Eloise mumbling, "Fat chance!" but Hannah faced him. "Sorry, Paul, but you couldn't keep up with any of us. Besides, we'd be afraid of catching something from you. There's got to be a problem, the way you keep scratching it." She heard Barbara snicker but kept watching Paul. If it had been possible, his eyes would have turned neon red, they were so full of rage. And just as quickly, he cooled down and smiled.

"You're just jealous, Hannah. Admit it. You're sorry you're involved with m'friend, Martin." He looked around the big room. "Why isn't he here yet? He usually gets here before I do."

"We're not *involved*, and you should be glad he's not here yet, or you'd be going out back all right. And it wouldn't be pleasant!"

"You don't know anything!" he said, smirking.

I'll bet I do, she thought.

Just then Martin came in the front door and Paul sauntered away.

"How disgusting!" June said. "Why does Martin put up with him?"

Hannah shrugged. "It just worked out that way. Can you imagine Paul working with Bob or Brad?"

"Hah! He wouldn't last one minute with either one of them."

Janet Litherland

"Well, Martin's tough. He can handle it."

"Let's get busy," Barbara suggested. "We have a lot to do today."

At the end of the work day, Martin and Hannah left the building together. Oddly, Martin was carrying a small bag containing a few grocery items.

"Martin?" Hannah pointed to the bag. "What's that for?"

"Oh!" He smiled. "It's not for me, if that's what you think."

"I hope not," she said, returning his smile.

He shook his head. "No. I'm dropping it off for an elderly gentleman over on Stark Street. He couldn't make it in today and asked if I could deliver. I figured it might be a nice gesture." *Sounds reasonable enough*, Hannah thought, though she couldn't remember a volunteer ever doing that.

"See you soon, I hope," Martin said with a wink. Then he waved and headed for his car.

Hannah knew that several of the food bank's "regulars" lived in the Stark Street area—a very poor section of town, populated by the underprivileged—but she didn't know the addresses of any of the folks who came to the food bank each month. She walked slowly to her car, pretending to search for keys in her purse; but she was stalling until Martin left the parking lot. She waited a couple of minutes longer before starting her car.

Her next moves were slow and deliberate. She drove to a street that crossed Stark approximately in the middle; and, as her car crept across, she looked both ways, hoping she could spot Martin's vehicle. She did. It was parked in a driveway two blocks to her right. Directly across the street from his car was a large old house painted a garish shade of yellow—a landmark. Satisfied, she kept going, away from the area.

She felt despondent all the way home. It had been five days since Martin said he was falling in love with her, and it seemed they'd been avoiding each other ever since. Obviously, she had not responded in the way he'd expected—she hadn't responded at all. Not because she

150

didn't want to. Oh, no! She had wanted very much to pretend the prickly problem growing like a fungus between them did not exist, so that she *could* accept his love. And even return it. But her head overruled her heart. She had kept quiet.

She was disappointed, too, because Martin hadn't shown any interest in her two-day trip to the antique show in Perry with her friends. If he cared about her, wouldn't he at least have asked about it? Stubborn, she refused to bring it up. Now, his odd visit to a house on Stark Street and his questionable explanation for it.

She picked up the evening paper from the front porch floor and took it inside. More depressing news: a front-page article on Georgia's unstable economy and weak job market. And, in just a few days the price of a first-class postage stamp would go up to thirty-seven cents! *Will it never end? I need something to lift my spirits!*

Hannah's first thought was a glass (or two or three!) of wine; but she had something important to do tonight and needed a clear head. So she settled for iced tea and a granola bar. … And she waited.

Chapter 25

After dark, Hannah went back to Stark Street and drove slowly toward the ugly yellow house. As she proceeded forward, she noted the address of her target across the street. The place was old and weathered, paint was chipped and several pieces of the porch railing were missing. A single lamp glowed from somewhere in the back of the house. There was no one outside—in fact, no sign of life in any of the yards or on porches along the street. The sight was depressing; and, being there, made her grateful once again to be part of the community-wide effort to provide for the needy. *No one should go hungry,* she thought, *and no one should be homeless!* She knew that many non-Jews were left homeless after the war, because their means of earning a living had dried up. Her eyes welled with tears, as she remembered her childhood friends left behind in Germany. Hannah wished there were more that could be done to solve the current homeless problem, a problem that existed in every city and town throughout the world.

Though it was late when she returned home, she hadn't eaten. So she put a frozen dinner in the microwave. She was grateful that she had food to eat, a comfortable place to live, and a warm, dry bed.

That night she fell asleep wondering why Martin had allowed her to see him leaving the food bank with that bag of food. Was this another carefully orchestrated slip? She was sure of it. But why? Was he suckering her into something she should be avoiding? Still, she knew she would follow up on it. She had to. Since the food bank was open only on Mondays and Thursdays, Hannah would have to wait until Monday for access to the database to see which client lived at the address she had memorized.

Next morning, Friday, Martin was at the gym, his usual friendly self, and they made plans to attend a movie on Saturday afternoon. After the movie, they walked in the park and bought sandwiches from a vendor—both of them ignoring the fact that he'd said he loved her.

"Martin, were you able to contact Art Lansfeldt's brother?" she asked as they sat on a park bench.

"I called the city morgue," he replied. "The brother's name is Ralph, and he had already claimed the body. There won't be any kind of memorial in Meadow Bridge, because no one really got to know Art. It's a shame, really. But I guess it was his own fault."

First Emily, now another one disappears without a trace.

~~~~~

They went to church on Sunday. The weather was beautiful—sunshine, with a few puffy white clouds in the sky. It reminded Hannah of one of her favorite John Denver lyrics, "Sunshine on my shoulders makes me happy." But she wasn't very happy right now. Anne was in the choir, and Hannah was back in "Charley" mode. After the service, Martin asked Hannah, "Shall we have lunch together?"

"Yes, but I really don't want to sit in a restaurant on this beautiful day. Let's get some takeout and go to one of those picnic tables in the park."

He raised an eyebrow. "We ate in the park yesterday, and today we're wearing church clothes. Not exactly dressed for a picnic."

"You can leave your suit coat in the car. And I'm wearing flat shoes—no heels to worry about."

He grinned. "Not letting me off the hook, are you?"

"Pretty please?" she asked, smiling.

"How can I possibly say no to that?"

They picked up salads at a deli and found a table in the shade of a large oak tree. Martin not only left his suit coat in the car, he tossed his tie in with it. They were both comfortable.

"Now tell me why we're here," Martin said, as he put a straw in his drink. "I can tell you have more on your mind than the sunshine."

"I want to talk without distractions. But let's eat first. I'm hungry."

"Uh-oh, sounds serious." He poked a fork into his salad and took a bite, while Hannah put artificial sweetener in her iced tea.

They weren't entirely quiet, making the usual small talk about the church service. They agreed that Anne Hargesty was a nice person and a good addition to the choir. After they finished eating, Martin gathered their papers and cups and took them to a nearby trash can. When he returned to the table, he glanced all around the area, then said, "Okay, no distractions. Everyone seems to be at the other end of the park. What is it, Hannah?" He took his seat across the table.

She looked straight at him, her eyes soft and kind. "First, I haven't forgotten that you said you might be falling in love with me. I have to tell you, Martin, that I feel the same. I *think* I'm falling in love with you." Actually, she knew for certain. She had finally, after many days of juggling Good, Bad, Love, Hate, Like, Cherish, and other contradictions in her usually logical mind, she'd given up. No matter what he was, past or present, she loved Martin Wynn. But she couldn't tell him now. Probably not ever.

A smile appeared on his face and he reached across the table as if to take her hands, but she pulled hers away. And his smile disappeared.

"You *think* you're falling in love with me … but …?" he asked.

"But we have important things to discuss before we can even consider talking about love."

"Like what?"

She smiled, but her tone was deadly serious. "I think you know," she said.

Martin sighed heavily. "Yes, I do know. Are you sure you want to have this conversation?"

"It's absolutely necessary, Martin."

"Then I'll make this easy for you," he said, "because I love you. I don't *think* I love you, Hannah. I *do* love you. I love you very much."

"... And that's supposed to make this *easier* for me?"

"You and I are kindred spirits. We could have been great partners, Hannah, in work as well as in life. We played the same game for years, just played for different teams."

Hannah swallowed hard and fought for composure. This conversation was her idea, and she wanted to control it. "I know you're a sleeper. How did you know about me?" she asked. "Were you sent here especially to find me?"

He shook his head slowly back and forth. "No," he said. "I discovered it on my own. I've told no one."

She lifted her chin and challenged him. Her tone was strong. "What was my mistake?"

"There was no mistake. As I said, we're kindred spirits. Because of what I am—and the fact that I was developing feelings for you—I became sensitive to everything about you, what you said and what you did. I wanted to know more about you. And, as we got to know each other better, I recognized techniques you were using to learn more about me, techniques that I, too, have used. I'm the one who made mistakes, Hannah. I was careless several times. I shouldn't have shown such an interest in the photo of your parents. As soon as I did, I knew I'd blundered, but I kept crossing my fingers, as if that would help. I shouldn't have taken you to meet my friends, Jeff and Shelly Karroll, after I'd suspected you were a retired agent. The Karrolls, regardless of what else they may be, really are my friends. I like them, and I wanted you to like them too."

"I do like them. Very much. I just don't like what they are. Or is it just one of them? Shelly?"

"Both," he said. "She recruited him. *Before* they were married. They do love each other."

"Were you planning to recruit me?"

"I wasn't planning anything, just living blindly day to day, like a dumb guy in love."

Hannah shook her head. "I guess I was doing the same. My times with you were—are—so enjoyable that I've tried very hard *not* to think about who or what you might be. All I wanted to do was prove my suspicions wrong. ... But I couldn't. You *are* a sleeper." She had no intention of telling him that she had come out of retirement to focus on him as a *job*.

"Well then, my dear, why don't we go on as we were? You stay retired and I'll stay asleep. We won't give another thought to our pasts." He reached across the table, and this time she put her hands in his.

"That would be very nice," she said, managing to smile even while thinking, *But I'm not retired right now, and you're no longer sleeping. You're working. We're both liars.*

"Just two more questions," she said, "before we close the subject. If you had known for certain about me earlier, would you have tried to recruit me?"

He studied her face for a moment before answering. "No, Hannah. There's a tough woman underneath your sweetness, and I would have known you couldn't be broken. You care too much about this country and the work you've done for it. Incidentally, I believe I know why you did it. It was about the War, wasn't it? And about what happened to your parents."

"Yes," she said, nodding proudly. "As I'm sure you've known since seeing the photo of my parents—my mistake for leaving it on the mantle—my mother was German and my father was a German Jew. Both of them died at Auschwitz, but not before arranging to have me safely transported out of the country. I was eight years old then, and I grew up in England near a USAAF base. When the war ended, I was so grateful to all of the Allies—especially the

Americans—that I knew I wanted to join them, to work for them."

Martin looked straight at her. "As I said, Hannah, if I'd known about you earlier, I would not have tried to recruit you. And, as I came to suspect and then to *know* what you are, there was no question of it."

"And what if I had tried to recruit you? Would you have considered it?"

He shook his head. "No, I would not have. But I'm sorry to say that my reason for declining would not be as noble as yours. I'm not particularly dedicated to the country I represent—rather, to its *regime*—but I *am* interested in self-preservation. Right now, sleeping in Meadow Bridge is my only option; and, I have to admit, it's a pretty good life." He squeezed her hands. "It led me to you."

~~~~~

That night Hannah considered her situation. Martin had said, plainly, that he loved her. She believed him. She also loved him, but they had no future together—too many loopholes and possible leaks, not the least of which would be his fellow sleepers. And what if Martin were truly activated, *wakened* by his regime? Where would that leave her? *In big trouble, that's where! To try is to die.*

She wished she could discuss it with someone, anyone; but that wouldn't be possible. The only person in Meadow Bridge she trusted enough to even *consider* confiding in was Eloise, but she couldn't risk her friend's life by putting that heavy burden on her shoulders. Her best choice of confidante—the choice that made the most sense—would be Trudi; but that, too, was impossible. Telephoning her was out of the question—too risky—and there was no way Hannah could come up with a reason for visiting Trudi on the spur of the moment. In fact, this year's biennial trip to Amsterdam was supposed to have taken place this week, but with her mission still incomplete, she'd had to postpone it indefinitely. Fortunately, Trudi understood, without needing to know why.

Chapter 26

Monday was not Hannah's day to work at the food bank, but she went in to check the database. It also was not Martin's day to work there, so he wouldn't be around to ask questions. Nor would Paul Smith be there.

Monday's women volunteers sometimes swapped places with Thursday's workers, so Hannah knew some of them. A woman named Mary was there on this day and greeted her as she entered.

"You subbing for someone today, Hannah?" Mary asked.

"No, just here to check the database. I was thinking about Mrs. Jones over the weekend and realized I hadn't seen her for a while," Hannah said. The lie came easily. "She's such a sweetheart; I want to call and make sure she's all right."

"Oh. Which Mrs. Jones is that? We've got several, you know."

Hannah nodded. "That's the problem. I'm not sure of her first name, but I've heard it before, and I'll know it when I see it. Don't let me keep you from your work!" Hannah smiled and scurried into the small, empty office.

When she'd told Doc and Laura that she wasn't into online networking, she'd told the truth. She'd also told them she had a computer and knew how to use it. That, too, was true. It took only seconds for her to find that Adrian Fortier lived at 42 Stark Street and had a local phone number. Yes, he was a food bank client, but Hannah had no memory of him. More than a thousand families depended on that particular charity every month, and knowing every individual by name would be impossible. She did note that Adrian Fortier usually picked up his groceries, but he'd missed a few times during the past year. Was he chronically ill? Did Martin, or someone else, take food to him? Or, was Adrian Fortier a false identity with a fake illness? *More questions.* In case Mary appeared and looked over her shoulder, Hannah pulled up all of the Joneses in the system. She sat there for several minutes, contemplating the Fortier situation. Then she closed the program and left the office.

"Did you find your Mrs. Jones?" Mary called, as Hannah passed by.

"Yes, and I'll ask about her. Have a great day, Mary!" She waved to some of the other workers and then went out the door.

Adrian Fortier. A Frenchman, Hannah thought. *More "cover" language? I wonder just how French he is. Born in France? Born here?* She decided to give him a call at the number she'd memorized. But to protect herself, she would use a public phone at the bus station.

She bought a cup of watery coffee from a vending machine and settled into the booth. After three rings an accented voice on the other end said, "*Allo?*" It was female.

Hannah responded with a question. *"Puis-je parler avec Monsieur Fortier?"*

"Qui etes-vous?" She wanted to know who Hannah was.

"Mon nom est ... Marie DuBois," Hannah replied, and she continued speaking in French, spinning a story. "I was involved in a minor accident in front of Mr. Fortier's house on Sunday afternoon. One of the neighbors said he may have seen it happen. I'd like to ask him about it."

"He is ill. He could not possibly have seen anything."

"Are you his nurse?"

"We cannot help you. Goodbye." And the connection was severed.

The woman had said Fortier was ill, which was also what Martin had claimed. But there was something disturbing about the short conversation. The speaker was not a native of

France. Her French was accented; and, to Hannah's practiced ear, the accent was Russian.

~~~~~

"Missed you at the gym this morning," Martin said when Hannah answered the phone.

"Thanks. I missed being there. I really needed the workout, especially after our lazy—but interesting— weekend. My list of errands was just too long to put off another day." *I'm a liar like you,* she thought. *I was checking on you and your Frenchman, or French*woman, *Adrian Fortier.* "Oh, Martin, I meant to ask you. Did that man appreciate the delivery last week?"

"What man?"

"The old gentleman. You took him a bag of food; said he lives on Stark Street."

"Oh … yes. He was very appreciative. He hadn't been feeling well."

"Have I met him? What's his name?" she asked, casually. "Maybe I can be of help in the future."

"It's Fortier. Adrian Fortier. I don't know whether you'd remember him."

"Maybe I would. What does he look like?"

"Are you checking up on me again, Hannah?"

She faked a laugh. "Sorry. Old habits are hard to break. But, no, I'm sincerely interested in helping."

"Believe me, I understand about old habits. Fortier is quite elderly; painfully thin; gray hair, what there is of it. But he has a nice smile and good manners."

That describes more than half our male clients, Hannah thought. *Thanks for nothing.* "Doesn't ring any bells," she said. "Fortier. Sounds French."

"Yeah, but he's been here in the states since he was a child, and he told me he never traveled much. I visit with him every once in a while, and we practice our French together. So, Hannah. I wish I could take you to dinner tonight, but some of the guys have invited me to play poker."

Nice change of subject. "That's great, Martin! You need to have more of those 'guy nights.' They're good for you."

"Maybe tomorrow night?"

"Maybe. If I'm not having a girl night!"

They both laughed. "I'll call you," he said.

But the call she got first thing Tuesday morning was from Doc.

"Of the names you gave us, four were cleared: Anne Hargesty, plus the golfers—Hanson, Calhoun, and Alcott. The others—Smith, Lansfeldt, Krenshaw and her Polos, the Karrolls, and of course Wynn—will be swept. By the way, you gave me two dead ones."

"What?"

"Rachel Krenshaw died in a house fire as a toddler in Gilles, Montana, in 1954 along with her parents and an older brother. Your 'Krenshaw-with-a-K' is a fake. She and her hardworking little cell of subversives—yes, they definitely are that—will no longer be recruiting and plotting against this country. By the way, the Polos are not connected to Wynn's sleeper cell."

Hannah was relieved, and glad she'd dug up the Polos. She assumed the other deceased whom Doc had referred to was Art Lansfeldt, but he surprised her.

"I said there were two 'dead' ones. The other is Richard Morrison. There are several Richard Morrisons in the U.S. but only two with that exact birth date. One is the mayor of a small town in Minnesota, and has been for years. Elected over and over. The other was one of four teenagers who stole a plane in 1960 and flew it into a dense mountain range in Idaho. Apparently, the plane incinerated on impact and no identifiable remains were recovered. Richard Morrison was declared dead. You have some explaining to do, Hannah."

After a long silence, she said, "There's one more. Art Lansfeldt is dead."

"What happened?"

"Motorcycle accident."

"How convenient."

"What do you mean by that?"

"Are you sure it was an accident? Maybe Lansfeldt was a liability."

Hannah felt sick. She'd already suspected Art was purposely eliminated. Now Doc suspected it too. She fervently hoped that Martin was not involved.

"At any rate," Doc said, "we're ready to bring the rest of them in, ASAP, and I want to hear about your Richard Morrison."

Hannah took a deep breath. "Later. And, Doc, hold off a little longer on the sweep. I have another name for you." She closed her eyes. *This is truly the end for Martin,* she thought.

"I'm listening."

"It's an old man. His name is Adrian Fortier."

"Hmm."

"Hmm, what?"

"You sure you don't mean Adrienne Four*nier*, a woman in her thirties?"

Hannah's heart sank. "I guess that's for you to find out." She gave him the Stark Street address and quickly disconnected. Again, Doc had been a step ahead of her. What the *hell* did he need her for?

Two things she was glad to have learned from Doc. The golfers were cleared, including Betty's husband, George. And Anne Hargesty was exactly what she'd claimed, a lonely widow in need of a friend. Hannah wished she could be that friend, but her happy life in Meadow Bridge would be ending soon. She was sure of it.

Paul Smith, Jeff and Shelly Karroll, and Rachel and her little band of devils were definitely dirty, as Art Lansfeldt had been. Those people were going down. And possibly others. Along with Martin Wynn, aka, Richard Morrison.

~~~~~~

Martin called later that day, as he'd promised, and asked her to dinner. But she declined. "Sorry," she said. "I told you I might have a girls' night out, and I do. My neighbor, Suzy, and her sister Betty—you remember Betty from the book club? They've invited me to spend the evening with them at Suzy's, and I'm looking forward to it. By the way, how was your poker game last night?"

"I lost, big time."

"How much?"

"Ten bucks. We were playing for quarters."

"That's big time all right. Win it back, and you can spend it on ice cream."

Their conversation ended genially, and Hannah got ready for the evening. She'd told Martin the truth. She really was having a girls' night out. Suzy had specified comfy clothes, so Hannah put on her favorite pair of jeans and a T-shirt that read, "High Maintenance." *Martin would get a laugh out of that*, she thought. Then she straightened. *But we won't have any more opportunities for laughs, will we?*

Chapter 27

Suzy had prepared an excellent dinner salad, with fresh vegetables and grilled steak sliced very thin. "This is scrumptious!" Hannah said. "Did you do the steak outside, Suzy? I thought I smelled it cooking a little while ago."

"Out back on my grill," she answered proudly. "And the vegetables are from my little garden, such as it is, taking up most of my back yard."

"You know our Suzy," Betty said. "She'd rather have a garden than grass!"

That was true. Suzy loved gardening and television, which didn't leave her much time for reading books. Her sister was the opposite. Betty loved to read, participated enthusiastically at the book club meetings, and proudly claimed to have the tallest *weeds* in Meadow Bridge!

The three women enjoyed one another's company, and Hannah thought about how much she'd miss them, and all of her other friends, when she disappeared within the next few weeks ... or days. Then she had an idea, something she could do to help Anne Hargesty, particularly if she—Hannah— were no longer around.

"I have a new friend," she said, as the evening was drawing to a close. "She's been in Meadow Bridge for several months but hasn't developed any real friendships. She volunteers at the animal shelter and loves the animals, but she's a bit shy when it comes to people. I met her in church, only because Martin and I spoke to her first. Then I took her to lunch one Sunday and found that I really like her.

The reason I'm telling you this is because I know you would understand her situation, especially you, Suzy."

"Me?"

Hannah nodded. "You and Betty and I have talked before about your marriage and the sad way it ended."

"For me, it went from sad to mad!" Suzy said. "Suddenly walking out on us like that, and for some floozy." She shook her head in disgust.

"Well," Hannah continued, "my friend—her name is Anne—her entire marriage was bad. Her husband was abusive, emotionally and physically. One day she ran away and ended up here in Meadow Bridge, where she didn't know a soul. Then she learned that he'd been killed in a car accident. She told me she felt guilty because she was glad he was dead. Anyway, that's why she hasn't made many friends—she's ashamed of being an abused wife."

"I was ashamed of my situation too," Suzy said. "At first. But then I toughened up. I realized I had nothing to be ashamed of. *He's* the one who should feel ashamed, not that he ever will. Your friend needs to get tough too!"

"Maybe we can help her. I was hoping the three of us could get together with Anne—perhaps over lunch one day soon—and encourage her to feel better about herself, regain her confidence. In the process, both of you might find a new friend too. What do you think, Betty? Suzy?"

They liked the idea very much and began making plans, and Hannah went home feeling relieved. She really did want to do something good for Anne. Maybe this was it. It could also be good for Suzy and Betty.

She fell asleep that night thankful that during her years in Meadow Bridge, which might soon be coming to an end, she had been able to make a difference in at least a few lives. She was glad her friendship with Eloise had provided a safe place for Eloise to vent, to relieve the pressure of impatience that often built up inside her. She recalled consoling Suzy when her husband left her and the children, and how their friendship had grown. She was happy that she had given

Anne the courage to join the church choir, and that Suzy and Betty would now take her under their warm wings. And working with the food bank—that wonderful charity not only continued to help many families each month, it also had helped Hannah realize how blessed she was. In Meadow Bridge she had redeemed and rebuilt her own life; and, in doing so, perhaps she *had* made a difference!

She spent the next day at home, doing laundry and reading—trying to concentrate on happy things rather than the problems and decisions now facing her. It wasn't easy. Finally, reluctantly, she got ready for bed.

Still no word from Doc.

~~~~~

Next morning Hannah went to the food bank with her nerves in shreds. Martin was working alongside the obnoxious Paul Smith. However, as Hannah took her place beside Eloise, her friend spoke quietly to her. "Did you hear that one of our clients passed away Tuesday night?"

"No, I didn't. Who was it?"

"His name was Fortier, that's all I know. I never saw him myself. Did you know him?"

Hannah's breath caught in her throat. "Uh … no, not at all. I'm sorry to hear that. What was the cause of death?"

Eloise shrugged. "Not a clue."

Hannah had a sick feeling in the pit of her stomach. "Do you know when or where the funeral service will be held?"

She shook her head. "No. We'll probably see an obituary in tomorrow's paper."

Probably not, Hannah reflected. Doc had taken care of business. She was sure of it. And whether it was the old man Adrian, or the younger woman Adrienne, or both, didn't matter. Doc and his kind didn't make mistakes. But someone at the food bank had made a *big* mistake. Or maybe it was intentional. Recipients were carefully screened, so how did Adrian Fortier end up in the database? Who had tampered with it? And did it again, so that it now read, *deceased*? Was it Martin? Or Paul Smith? And why was Fortier the only one picked up? Why hadn't the others been taken at the same time? Hannah excused herself and went outside to use her secure cell phone.

"You did it, didn't you?" she asked.

"Um-hmm. Good work, Hannah," Doc answered.

"Fortier was an old man. Old and sick."

"The old man didn't exist. It was a cover for Adrienne. The woman was an active foreign agent. I stress the word *was*," he added with a touch of pride. "She was not French—she was Russian—and Fournier was an assumed name. However, we got an anonymous tip early Tuesday morning, a damn good one, supplying the name, Adrienne Fournier—aka Adrian Fortier—with a couple of intriguing and undeniable details. Then you called with the same name and confirmed the address in Meadow Bridge. The team chose to act on it immediately, before Adrienne decided to run."

Got the tip on Tuesday morning, Hannah thought. *After Martin and I had talked about "Mr. Fortier." So he had known Adrienne Fournier, had covered for her, and had visited her, probably many times. Were they more than just comrades? Or, could he have phoned in the tip? Did he suddenly turn against her? Why?*

Doc continued. "Your friend, Rachel—"

She interrupted, "Rachel Krenshaw is *not* my friend."

"Rachel and the Polos, the Karrolls, Smith—we're bringing them all in tonight. Too bad somebody else got to Lansfeldt first. And, Hannah, we're taking Martin Wynn in, too. Every bit of intel you gathered for us, no matter how insignificant it may have seemed, was important, especially meeting the Karrolls. If you hadn't wormed your way into Wynn's heart—if he has one—he never would have let you meet them, and we would not have known about them."

"His heart, *if he has one? Wormed* my way in? You don't know much about me, Doc!" She wished she could throw the phone down and stomp on it!

"I know that you'll do the job, whatever it takes. And, Hannah, you *are* in a unique position to accomplish exactly what needed done. You've uncovered the cell, not to mention the Polos. And now you've given us Wynn's telltale visit to Adrienne Fournier. Adrienne knew there were other cell members, but she—like the others—didn't know who belonged and who didn't. She admitted this, shall we say, under duress? Wynn is the *only* one connected to all of the others. That's enough to confirm our initial tip from the defector—Martin Wynn is a leader. Now tell me, Hannah, what I already suspect. Is Richard Morrison one of Wynn's aliases?"

It was time. "Yes. I found a forged driver's license locked in the glove box of his car."

"Were you ever going to tell me?"

"Of course I was! That was one reason for calling you just now," she lied.

"Hmmph. I still say, 'Good work, Hannah.' Our teams are prepared to make the arrests. Tonight."

Hannah's voice was filled with anger. "But, Doc, I called *you* just now!" she said. "You weren't going to tell me, were you?"

"Back at you, Hannah. You would have been told, but only after the fact."

"Unacceptable. I want to be there when they pick up Martin," Hannah said.

"Do you think that's wise?"

"It's important to me."

"It has to be tonight. He's certainly on alert now. Unless he's so smitten with you that he doesn't care anymore," Doc added.

Hannah couldn't miss the facetious tone of his voice. Still, she had to try. "Then give him—give *us*—a chance to say goodbye. You said he might be 'smitten' with me. Yes, he is; and I still have enough kindness left in my tough old heart that I don't want to trample on his feelings.

Professionally, we're worlds apart; but personally, Martin and I have had many good times together."

"If we wait, he's going to figure it out. Wynn has been 'sleeping' for several years, but he's not stupid."

That hurt. "I'll invite him to my house for dinner this evening, seven o'clock. Give us time alone first. Please."

"You cannot warn him, Hannah," he said, a little stronger than necessary.

"I'm not stupid either, Doc."

"The team will be in place *before* seven. They'll give you ten minutes."

"Ten minutes! At least let us have dinner!"

"Thirty minutes. I'm feeling generous. One man will be stationed inside the house, just—"

Hannah interrupted him. "Oh, for heaven's sake, Doc! Martin isn't violent, and he'd never hurt me!"

"You don't know that."

She had to admit, there was a lot she didn't know, a lot she was learning, even at this stage in her life. "I don't want any of them inside my house. I can take care of myself!"

"Remember what I said a few days ago, Hannah. Your life is in danger!"

"After tonight, it won't matter, will it? My life in Meadow Bridge won't be worth a damn anyway."

She went back inside, made an excuse to Eloise, stopped at Martin's table, and pulled him aside. "My neighbor just called, reminding me that I'm supposed to pick her up for her dentist appointment in half an hour," she said. "Glad I'm not the patient. I'm allergic to pain!" Martin laughed, and she asked, "Want to come to my house for dinner this evening?"

"Beef stew again, Hannah?" he asked. She could hear the sweet smile in his voice, and it nearly broke her heart.

Still, she managed to sound cheerful. "Not this time! I'm baking lasagna, and there's always too much for one person. Can you be there at seven?"

"See you then."

She went home to prepare for the evening, the dreaded evening, feeling deceitful and ashamed.

Yet hadn't she, too, been deceived? And not only by Martin. She never could have imagined so many shady people hiding among the beautiful trees of her beloved Meadow Bridge. Of course she—Hannah—had also been hiding there, as Laura had sarcastically reminded her during her first meeting with Doc.

It had been thirty years since Charley Stowne had retired as Hannah Rosse, but she'd always been proud of being one of the good guys, even if the good guys sometimes had to do bad things. But tonight was different. This was Martin, and she had betrayed him. Martin Wynn, who had made her laugh—and love—again.

Chapter 28

"Dinner smells wonderful," Martin said, as Hannah opened the door for him. She then closed it, leaving it unlocked.

Martin looked especially handsome, even rugged, in jeans and a light blue polo shirt. He smiled as he gave her a quick hug. Then he pulled back and said, "Could we just relax here in the living room for a few minutes first?"

Hannah returned his smile. "I was going to suggest it. Would you like some Chianti? It just needs pouring."

He followed her to the kitchen, making small talk, and they returned to the living room with their wine. Then he motioned for her to sit next to him on the sofa and held up his glass for a toast. "To us," he said.

"To us," Hannah replied, knowing there would never be an "us." Her heart was breaking, and she was nervous. *Please don't let it show.* "Did you have a nice day, Martin?" she asked.

"Not especially. How about you?"

"No. Not really." She sipped her wine, wanting to put off the inevitable. "I suppose you wonder why I invited you here on the spur of the moment, on a Monday of all nights."

He slowly shook his head. "I don't wonder at all, Hannah. I know." His expression was somber, but kind.

"… You do?"

"Um-hmm." He carefully set his wine glass on the coffee table, took her glass and put it next to his, and then gently enfolded her hands in his.

"I told you earlier that I was the one who made mistakes. I have to say that a couple of them were intentional, like giving you the wrong day for the Kiwanis meeting in Perry. I fantasized that we would suddenly confess our pasts to each other and just disappear together. But that was faulty, emotional thinking."

Hannah blinked. "I ... I had exactly the same fantasy, Martin. I called it 'riding off into the sunset.'"

He smiled and squeezed her hands. "It never would have been possible," he said, gently. "I retreated from my intentional mistake by telling you I'd had the Kiwanis meeting days mixed up. But I was *careless* when you saw me with the bag of food, headed for Stark Street."

"For Adrian Fortier? Or should I say Adrienne Fournier? You're not just a liar, Martin Wynn." Then she added, softly, "You're a *damn* liar."

He replied with equal softness, "It was my job, and you, of all people, should understand that."

"Why did you go there?" She couldn't bear the thought that Martin and Adrienne might be more than just comrades.

"I talked with all of my people frequently—Art at the book club meetings, Paul at the food bank, Jeff and Shelly at their farm. There are also two others. You don't know them," he added to reassure her. "I'll give them up, too. Your folks can make it a complete sweep." He cleared his throat. "As for Adrienne, she is the only one I didn't see on a regular basis. She kept to herself, did not try to make friends or get involved in the community, didn't talk much, and never smiled." Then Martin smiled, lifted Hannah's hands and planted a kiss on her fingertips. "That's all there was to Adrienne, Hannah. Just business." He sighed. "I'd often wondered why she'd been sent here. Maybe it was to keep tabs on me."

"Maybe."

"But know this: Going to Stark Street was *not* an intentional slip. It was something I had done many times before, unnoticed. You'd bewitched me."

"You tampered with the database?"

He nodded. "But then you caught on. I was watching from an upstairs window at the house that afternoon, hoping I wouldn't see you. I wanted you to be *anything* other than what you were." He released one of her hands, just long enough to take a rather large drink of wine. Then he carefully returned his glass to the table and retrieved her hand. "I saw your car cross Stark Street, which was exactly what I would have done if I'd been in your situation." He paused, taking a deep breath. "That was the day I finally put it all together."

She was afraid to ask, but she had to know. "Put … put what together?"

"You really haven't changed much over the last thirty years, Hannah. Your hair is a different shade—the red is gone—and it's shorter, but that's about all. You're still about the same size, with the same bright smile and laughter. You've aged well."

She could only stare at him, could hardly breathe.

"I was there," he said. "In Northern Ireland. I was supposed to be protecting him, but you seemed harmless enough, just a fun-loving little Irish girl. Then, when the merrymaking settled down, he was dead and you were gone. It looked like he'd had a drunken accident. That's what everyone thought. I knew better, but I was too cowardly to admit I'd used bad judgment." He sighed. "I always wondered what had happened to you."

Hannah remained frozen. Her hands were in his, nowhere near her pocket.

He sensed her fear. "Relax, Hannah. I could never hurt you; I love you too much." He gave her hands another gentle squeeze, then released them. "After realizing who you were, I was very glad I had not tried to recruit you. If I had, and you didn't kill me, my organization would have, for making a fool of myself—of *them*—by not recognizing who and what you were. And for not doing my job. The situation had to remain an 'accident,' though I did receive a severe reprimand for letting the guy get drunk. Yesterday, as soon as I discovered Adrienne had been taken, I could have—and probably *should* have—left Meadow Bridge, just walked away. I knew I'd be next."

"Did you … Were you the one who called in the tip? About her?"

He nodded. "I purposely set up my own downfall," he said.

"I have some questions."

"Anything at all."

"Why so many French speakers? You, Emily, Shelly, Adrienne?"

"Emily and Shelly were both born in France and grew up there. Adrienne is Russian and began working for her country's regime in France, as I did. None of us knew the others until arriving in the U.S. The language bond was coincidence." He took another drink, a smaller one this time. "More questions?"

She nodded. "What really happened to Art Lansfeldt?"

"You don't believe it was an accident?"

She shook her head. "No."

He sighed. "Adrienne arranged it and informed me after it was over. She resented my leadership. Over time, her mood would swing from hostile to indifferent. She finally went rogue. She didn't know Art or any of the others, but she'd somehow discovered he was a fellow sleeper—maybe through another of my mistakes." He shook his head regretfully. "She'd been watching him and decided on her own that he was a liability. Problem was, she had no authority to make that decision." He paused. "That's why I called in the tip about her. I decided *she* was a liability and that would be a good way to get rid of her without getting *rid* of her, if you know what I mean. And, like I said, I knew I'd be next."

"Who really claimed Art's body?"

"I did. One of my aliases was 'Ralph Lansfeldt.' Forged documents and a disguise eliminated any questions. As ordered, I had the body shipped to a mortuary in Indiana. Where it went from there, no one will ever know. I did the same thing with the body in Northern Ireland all those years ago, had it shipped to a place in Germany where it disappeared."

Hannah straightened her shoulders. "Who shot a bullet through my living room window, and why?"

He closed his eyes and held them shut for a few seconds.

"Don't lie to me, Martin."

"No lies." His eyes opened, and his expression was weary. "It was Adrienne. She told me about it when she confessed to killing Art. She was proud of both acts of violence, I might add. Why did she shoot into your home? She'd seen us together many times and believed I was being distracted from my job—the job she felt should have been hers."

"She didn't shoot to kill."

"No. It was a warning—a warning to *me*, not to you. She had no knowledge of your background; but she was sure, as a woman, you'd run to tell me about it. Then I would stop seeing you to 'protect' you. If I didn't stop seeing you, she'd report me as an ineffective operative. Personally, I believe her motive was envy of my position. As I said, that's when I called in the tip about her. She was a rogue and definitely a liability." He sighed, heavily. "I'm sorry if she scared you."

"She didn't. One more question. Was Emily an operative?"

"Yes."

"Did you ... did you kill her?"

"No," he answered quickly and earnestly. "I loved my wife. I told you the truth, Hannah. Emily's heart failed her."

A single tear escaped Hannah's eye, but she remained strong. "I want you to know one thing, Martin," she said, "and don't ever forget it. I do love you. I truly do."

"I know. ... It's hard to hide love." His eyes began to water. "I couldn't hide my love for you."

After a few quiet moments she asked, "Why didn't you leave Meadow Bridge days ago, Martin? Why didn't you walk away before it came to this?"

"My first thought, a programmed reaction, was to use my knowledge as leverage: 'Don't turn me in and I won't expose you.'" He shook his head. "But I couldn't do that because, as I said, I had fallen in love with you, Hannah. And remember this: I will never, ever reveal your past. It's safe with me. I came here tonight knowing what will happen, because I wanted to see you once more. And because it's time. I'm tired of the game. I want to go home."

"Home to Russia?"

He sighed and blinked a few times, dispensing the unshed tears. "I wish I could go to my *real* home ... in England. I'm British, Hannah, not Russian. I trained at Beaulieu, but back then I was a naïve kid who thought he could learn more from working both sides of the street. I was caught by the other side. They turned me, using vicious threats against my parents and my little sister. I honestly believed I had no choice, if I wanted to save my family. Fortunately, I've been able to contact them a few times over the years, clandestinely of course. Even met with them once in Belgium, after my little sister was a grown woman." His smile was sad. "So, yes, I'm going 'home' to Russia, such as it is. Your people will arrest me tonight, and I'll be deported. Probably exchanged for one of yours. That's the way things are done now."

Just then the front door opened, and two armed agents stepped into the room.

"You won't need your guns," Martin said, looking up. He stood and held his hands out in front of him. As the cuffs were put on his wrists, he looked back at Hannah, who remained seated. "Have no regrets, Hannah. You did what you had to do. I just didn't realize it would happen so early in the evening," he said. "I'd hoped ... I'd hoped we'd have more time together. ... Our last time together." The sadness on his face was heartbreaking.

"Martin," she said, a tear sliding down her cheek, "You, also, did what you had to do. For your family. I will always love the person you really are."

He swallowed hard, battling a tear of his own. "I feel the same about you, Hannah."

Without another word from anyone, he was gone. The door closed quietly, and Hannah sat for a long time in the stillness.

Eventually, she stood, walked to the door and locked it. Then she reached for the wine glasses to take to the kitchen. But there was something under Martin's glass—a small piece of brown paper, turned upside down. She snatched it up, glanced at the other side, and smiled. Then she took the wine glasses to the sink, turned off the oven and hurried upstairs, letting the lasagna shrivel.

Hannah went straight to her bedroom, kicked off her shoes, picked up the beloved music box Martin had given her, and curled up in the big soft chair near her bed. She wound the key to "The Music of the Night" and let it play as she studied Martin's brief message. It was a cipher. And Hannah Rosse was good at ciphers:

Y02-R26:21R198/

Chapter 29

Hannah had needed only twenty minutes to "decipher" Martin's cipher before burning it. It was really very simple. Her skills with codes and ciphers were obviously more advanced than his! She smiled all over, inside and out, just thinking about him. He'd said he would never betray her, and she knew he would not. When he was taken away, there was no denying his love for her, or hers for him, despite their extreme, incompatible, fixed loyalties. The message of the cipher: *This is not the end for us. Forever yours.* She had not seen the last of him!

Early the next morning Doc called to tell her that the sweep was successful and to "get the hell out of Meadow Bridge. Cleanup is on its way," he said, adding, "The Karrolls were especially interesting. They were growing more than melons on that farm."

"Let me guess. Marijuana?"

"Lots of it! Good job with this entire situation, Hannah. Thanks!"

She shook her head in dismay, glad the "situation" was finally over. She quickly took care of household chores and pulled a special travel bag out of her closet. During her adult life she had always kept a small bag packed with essentials—two changes of clothing and toiletries—to be ready to leave immediately whenever she was called. When she'd retired and moved to Meadow Bridge, she thought she'd never need it again, but as soon as John Jackson had left her front porch after talk of "one last job," she'd reassembled the travel bag. Just in case.

Now, she added a few special things to it—the photos of her parents and David; a few snapshots of friends and scenes in and around Meadow Bridge; her CIA medal, her special knife, and the Cricket; and the little music box Martin had given her. Because of the knife and the music box, she would have to check the bag at the airport rather than take it as a carryon. She wished she could take her puzzle-picture, but that was out of the question. In addition to the bag, she carried a purse large enough to hold a paperback book and some snacks. Then, a secure call to headquarters assured her that her remaining financial property would be transferred to Hanne Ashworth in Amsterdam.

When everything was in order, she notified her friends, neighbors, and the food bank volunteers that she would be away for a while—"family emergency." That included a call to her dear friend, Eloise, assuring her that she'd be back soon and they'd resume their lunches together—a lie, of course—one that made her weep. She also encouraged Suzy and Betty to call Anne Hargesty while she was gone. She really wanted those friendships to take root.

Within a short time she was on a plane to Amsterdam, just three weeks past the originally scheduled date for her biennial visit with Trudi. This visit would last a long time, probably for the rest of her life.

Though Hannah's feelings were mixed, she was mostly content. She would have a familiar identity—Hanne Ashworth—and she would be living with her beloved cousin in the countryside near Amsterdam, a place she adored. *What will my friends in Meadow Bridge think when I don't come back?* she wondered. *Or when they realize that Martin and Paul have disappeared too? Guess I'll never know. My house will be cleared and cleaned. Excuses will be made, and my "death" arranged. Why? Because there can be no trace. There will always be questions. And those questions can never be answered.*

~~~~~

"I'm so glad you're here, Hanne!" Trudi said, giving her cousin a big hug.

"You may not be so glad when I tell you how long I plan to stay."

Trudi's smile faded. "Oh, no! Just a short visit?"

"Afraid not. It's going to be a long one."

"Long? Yes! How long?"

"Is *forever* too long?"

After two seconds of stunned silence, Trudi burst into laughter and gave Hanne another hug, this time nearly knocking them both off balance. "Come in! Tell me!" she said. "We'll get your bags later."

Hanne had just arrived from the airport in her rental car—she had braved the bicycles—and they were walking toward Trudi's front door. "I have only one bag, and this is it." Hanne had her small travel case in one hand and her purse over the opposite shoulder. "You know I never take a lot of luggage."

Trudi's eyes widened. "Even for *forever*?"

"*Especially* for forever. I'm really starting over, Trudi."

They entered the house and sat together on the living room sofa. "Tell me!" Trudi said. "Don't leave anything out."

"Got something cold to drink?"

"Hanne!" But Trudi got up and dashed to the kitchen, laughing, returning with two filled glasses. "Now?"

Hanne couldn't help chuckling. "Okay." She took a long, slow sip of her drink.

"Hanne!"

"It's like this. ... I blew my own cover."

"...You? But ..."

"Yes, I did it. As you know, I was observing a foreign agent. What you don't know—and I didn't realize at first—is that he began observing me." She smiled. "And in the process, we fell in love."

"Hanne!"

Hanne laughed. "Quit shouting my name, Trudi. Don't you know one is never too old for love?"

"It's not that. You're not old anyway; at least you don't—*we* don't—seem old," she said. "But in love with a *foreign* agent? Have you lost your mind?"

"Maybe. Probably. But I'm not sorry. I successfully completed my mission—you and I have talked before about my being pulled from retirement—and I was satisfied with the outcome. Some bad people were removed from a very nice little town."

"Including your, uh ..."

"Yes, including him, though he wasn't really a bad man."

Trudi's eyes were questioning.

"It's complicated," Hanne said. "Anyway, after stirring things up, I had to leave too. Forever. That's why I'm here."

"I could not be happier! But what about him, your love?"

Hanne smiled. "I know in my heart that I will see him again—someday, sometime, somewhere."

Chapter 30

Exactly one year from the day she'd last seen Martin, Hanne was seated at a small table at her favorite outdoor café, watching boats on the canal, drinking fruit juice, and reminiscing. She'd never forget that sad night, when he was handcuffed and taken away, just seconds after they'd spoken of love. But more important, she'd never forget the good times they'd had—their dinners at Donnalee's, the walks in the park, the ice cream, their silly fun at Taco Bell, riding in that beautiful '57 Chevy, their romantic dinner in Macon where the string quartet had played "The Music of the Night," and the day Martin had given her the treasured little music box.

Now, she removed it from her purse, wound it, and set it on the café table in front of her. As the song played, Martin moved quietly up beside her. "May I join you?" he asked.

She was surprised; but, like a good former agent, she didn't show it. Except with her eyes. "Yes, please do." Her pulse and her breath quickened as he pulled out a chair and sat next to her. "It's beautiful here, isn't it?" she said, looking out over the water.

"Very beautiful," he said, looking directly at her.

She smiled and turned to him. "Same old line, and you're not even drinking."

"It's no line. You are beautiful, and you'll never change. Not in my eyes. It's good to see you, Hannah."

"Likewise. I've missed you, Martin."

"You are my one regret in life. I regret that we can never be a couple and enjoy our last years together."

"If we tried, neither of us would live very long."

"I know. If your people didn't get us, mine surely would," he said. "Because, together, neither side would trust us. Not ever again. This visit, of course, had to be secret."

"Life is not fair."

"No, it isn't. But I'm glad the exchange was made—a spy for a spy—and I could be here with you today, rather than in an American prison."

"Me, too."

"You knew I'd find you, didn't you?" She nodded. "But I promise you, Hannah, that no one else ever will. I was very careful to cover each track I made."

"I trust you, Martin." She smiled. "I didn't know when you'd come. I thought it *might* be today, since the date is significant to both of us."

It was his turn to smile. "I needed to erase that last memory and replace it with something better. Much better. Would you like to go for a boat ride?"

She stood and offered him her hand. And her heart.

They had a lovely afternoon, a romantic dinner by candlelight, and an unforgettable night. He left early the next morning.

And now they both had a beautiful memory to cherish.

Epilogue

Amsterdam, the Netherlands—2012

It has now been ten years since Hannah Rosse left Meadow Bridge and ceased to exist. Meadow Bridge is a wonderful memory of thirty very special years, but only a memory. During my lifetime I learned that one must live in the present, not the past nor the future. In just these last ten years as Hanne Ashworth, many innovations have affected the way people live in the present. I've seen the growth of social networking through Facebook and LinkedIn (I still don't indulge!); television databases such as Netflix; text messaging; GPS in autos; hybrid cars; telerobotic surgery; and much more. I'm glad I survived to see all of this.

Martin never again visited me in Amsterdam—too risky for both of us—but often over the years I heard from him anonymously. I could never reply, and that makes my heart ache.

Yesterday was my eightieth birthday, and I received something very special in the mail. No card, no note, no return address; just a large flat envelope with a sheet of music inside: "The Music of the Night." He had underlined the lyrics that tell me I'm the only one who can make his "song take flight." And he had added the words, "Only and forever." Martin is still alive, knows where I am ... and still loves me.

The night I betrayed Martin—the night he was taken away—I stayed awake for a very long time. Despite his

185

encouraging cipher, I felt deep guilt, shame, and sadness. I wondered if there were enough life, or will, left in me to bother starting over. Did I want to? I was still healthy, but I was tired and discouraged. However, if I had not chosen to start over, there was only one other option. Yes, I considered it. But when I reflected on my life and the good I had accomplished—which far outweighed the bad—and my reason for doing those things, my reason for surviving, I knew I would begin yet another new life. And this new life as Hanne Ashworth has been very good.

My beloved Mutti's last words to me were, "You must do whatever it takes to survive. Promise me!" I promised. And I will keep that promise, even to the end.

Danke für das Lesen meiner Geschichte. Ich musste es mir vom Herzen reden. Jetzt fühle ich, dass meine Seele rein ist. Endlich. (Thank you for reading my story. I had to get it off my chest. Now I feel that my soul is clean. Finally.)

Acknowledgments

I continue to be inspired by stories of World War II veterans—including my late father—who endured so much for freedom's sake, as our military has continued to do in years since. This story, though inspired by "the greatest generation," is a product of my imagination, and any resemblance to people living or dead is coincidental.

My sincere appreciation to the following, who were kind enough to read the final draft and offer helpful comments. Their input was invaluable: Bettina Krone, Betty Claire Neill, Eddie Smith, Betty Westley, Diana Williams, and Mark Litherland. Thank you!

It is said that writing is a lonely profession. Not for me. My family and friends continue to surround me with love and encouragement, for which I will be eternally grateful. May God bless all of you!